Soon she would be lifting bales of hay like they were ~~nothing~~

Leah put her hands on ~~her~~ in deep breaths. "I kno~~w~~ practice, but wow. You ~~were right. I feel~~ stupid for not thinking ~~it through.~~

Shane handed her a bottle of water. "Not stupid. Inexperienced. I know you think I've been hard on you, but I don't want you to fail simply because you hadn't thought everything through."

She nodded.

"You're smart and capable," he continued. "You have more grit and gumption than a lot of people I know. I understand why you don't trust easily. But I'm asking you to have a little faith in the fact that I'm here to help you. I made a promise to Helen, and I'm doing for you what Helen always wanted to do."

She brushed the hay off her pants. "I've given you more trust than I've given anyone else in a long time."

Shane didn't want to think about trust issues.

He hoped he could continue showing her that he had her best interests at heart…even when she didn't understand.

Danica Favorite loves the adventure of living a creative life. She loves to explore the depths of human nature and follow people on the journey to happily-ever-after. Though the journey is often bumpy, those bumps refine imperfect characters as they live the life God created them for. Oops, that just spoiled the ending of Danica's stories. Then again, getting there is all the fun. Find her at danicafavorite.com.

Books by Danica Favorite

Love Inspired

Three Sisters Ranch
Her Cowboy Inheritance

Love Inspired Historical

Rocky Mountain Dreams
The Lawman's Redemption
Shotgun Marriage
The Nanny's Little Matchmakers
For the Sake of the Children
An Unlikely Mother
Mistletoe Mommy
Honor-Bound Lawman

Visit the Author Profile page at Harlequin.com for more titles.

Her Cowboy Inheritance

Danica Favorite

HARLEQUIN® LOVE INSPIRED®

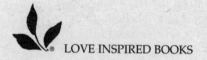

LOVE INSPIRED BOOKS

Recycling programs for this product may not exist in your area.

ISBN-13: 978-1-335-47898-6

Her Cowboy Inheritance

Copyright © 2019 by Danica Favorite

www.Harlequin.com

Printed in U.S.A.

Charity suffereth long, and is kind; charity envieth not; charity vaunteth not itself, is not puffed up, Doth not behave itself unseemly, seeketh not her own, is not easily provoked, thinketh no evil; Rejoiceth not in iniquity, but rejoiceth in the truth; Beareth all things, believeth all things, hopeth all things, endureth all things. Charity never faileth: but whether there be prophecies, they shall fail; whether there be tongues, they shall cease; whether there be knowledge, it shall vanish away.

—*1 Corinthians* 13:4–8

For all the moms out there who are
doing the best they can with what they have.
You've got this!

Chapter One

❧

Leah Holloway stood inside the old ranch house in Columbine Springs, Colorado, unable to believe that in the twenty years since she'd last been here, everything seemed almost unchanged. Except for the silence and emptiness.

"It's weird not seeing Grandma Nellie sitting in her rocking chair, isn't it?" her sister Erin said, coming behind her.

Leah turned. "She wasn't our grandmother."

"The closest thing we had to one. Besides, everyone called her Grandma Nellie." Erin put her arm around her and gave a squeeze. "You doing okay?"

Everyone asked her that, and Leah hated having to answer the question. Of course she wasn't doing okay. How could anybody be okay when everything in her life was falling apart? Everyone had a million questions for her, and Leah hadn't had the chance to process what had happened. She'd been too busy trying to stay strong for her kids, doing everything she could to keep a roof over their heads, and now this.

Not that being here on the ranch was necessarily a

bad thing, since the surprise bequest was literally the only reason she and her kids wouldn't be living on the streets. But it was one more set of emotions being thrown at her that she didn't have time to deal with.

Fortunately, her sister Nicole came in, carrying a box. "Isn't this great? I can't believe this is all ours."

Erin gave their sister a small smile. "The happiest I remember being as children was the summer we spent here with Helen. The Colonel was on another temporary assignment, and she brought us here to her family's ranch. I remember wishing we could stay here forever and never have to see the Colonel again. Who would have thought the wish of a ten-year-old would come true twenty years later?"

For a moment, Erin looked wistful, but then she shook her head. "It's crazy to think that Helen remembered us enough to leave us her family's ranch. I feel bad that we didn't stay in better touch with her."

Leah shrugged. "The Colonel would've never allowed it. Not with the way he threw her out. He thought she was a bad influence, allowing too much disorder in his household."

"I don't remember that," Nicole said. "I barely remember Helen at all. I still think it's weird that she left us her estate."

The lawyer had given them a letter from Helen, outlining the reasons for her bequest. They'd all read the letter, but Nicole, who had only been six when the Colonel had divorced Helen, hadn't responded to it the way Leah and Erin had. How could she? She'd been too young to understand so much of what had happened.

Unfortunately, Leah had been twelve, which meant

she had understood far too much. Nicole being so young had been a blessing.

Sometimes, it was the only thing that gave Leah hope that her sons, Dylan and Ryan, would come through their own family tragedy unscathed. At seven and two, they barely remembered their father, who'd emotionally checked out of their lives long before his death six months ago. In some ways, her sons' childhood mirrored so much of what Leah's had been that it scared her. She'd spent her whole life vowing to do things differently when she had children of her own. The only differences were Leah's mother had died when Nicole was a baby, and their father had been a monster. When the Colonel had died several years ago, she hadn't felt the level of grief she did now for Helen.

Leah would like to think that she was a reasonably good parent to her boys, even though their father had not been. Of course, she hadn't known the truth about him until it was too late.

A knock sounded at the door, and the three women turned. The silhouette of a cowboy was framed in the entryway, like one of those Western paintings you bought at tourist traps. As he stepped forward, he almost took Leah's breath away. So handsome, with his rugged good looks and dark hair that barely brushed the top of his collar. If she had to guess, she'd say he was near her own age, maybe a bit older. But looks could be deceiving, as she well knew, and she didn't have time to deal with whatever weird attraction this was. She couldn't even handle the real emotions flooding her.

"Hope I'm not intruding," the cowboy said. "I saw cars in front of the house when I came to check on my cattle, and I thought I'd introduce myself. I'm Shane Jackson, and I own the ranch next door."

The lawyer had mentioned something about Shane Jackson, but Leah couldn't remember what it was. Dylan had been throwing a fit, and Leah had been doing her best to calm him down.

Leah stepped forward. "It's nice to meet you. I'm Leah, and these are my sisters, Erin and Nicole. If you looked closely at the cars when you walked up, you might have noticed my sons, Dylan and Ryan, asleep in the backseat of the Subaru."

Shane shook his head. "I'm afraid not. The back door of the Subaru was open. I closed it, so no critters could get in. There were no children in there."

The air rushed out of Leah's lungs. The boys had to be in there. Ryan couldn't even get out of his car seat without help. She brushed past Shane and out of the house, running to her car. But as she drew near, her heart sank. The boys were gone.

What kind of mother was she, losing her children?

"They were asleep," Leah said, looking around. Where were her children?

Shane and her sisters had followed her, and immediately, Erin and Nicole started calling out for them.

"Clearly not," Shane said, obvious disapproval in his voice.

Who was this man, and what right did he have to question her parenting? The lawyer was probably warning her off about him, and she'd missed it.

"Boys!" Leah called, going to the other side of her car in case they were just hiding. "You're not in trouble. Mommy just needs to know where you are."

She fought to keep the panic out of her voice. Dylan

especially was prone to hiding when he thought he'd done something wrong. If he sensed she was upset, he'd make it even harder for them to find him.

Her sisters had split up and gone to either side of the house, so Leah ran toward the barn. Ryan's favorite toy was his plastic barn and animals. Maybe he'd seen the barn and hoped to find real animals, too.

Hopefully, the boys hadn't found anything too dangerous to get into.

When she got closer to the barn, she could see a horse tied to the far side. And the boys petting it.

"Dylan! Ryan!" As she shouted their names, Shane grabbed her by the arm.

"Stop yelling. You're going to scare my horse."

Who did he think he was, worrying about a horse when she'd thought she'd lost her sons?

He jogged a few steps forward, then slowed to a walk, holding out his arm to keep Leah from passing him.

"Hey!"

"Shh." He shot her a glare, then took another step forward. "Hey there, boys," he said in a soft voice. "Whatcha doing over here?"

"Petting da horse," Ryan said, touching the horse's leg.

It was almost sweet, watching her son fulfill his dream of being around horses. But even Leah knew that it wasn't safe for him to be there, touching the horse in that way.

"Easy, Squirt." Shane took a long step in the direction of the horse. "Steady."

The horse gave a toss of his head as if he understood Shane, and Shane took another giant step forward. If the horse lifted his leg or shifted his weight, he could easily step on the little boy. Dylan was standing farther back. At least one of her sons was safe. But even that wasn't a guarantee. Though it had been a long time since Leah had been around horses, she knew they spooked easily.

"Hey, boys, why don't you come stand by me, and I'll introduce you to Squirt properly."

Shane's voice was calm and gentle, and the boys looked at him. Then they saw Leah.

"I don't want to get in trouble," Dylan said, his lips quivering.

Shane shot her a dirty look. What was with him and his judgmental attitude? He didn't know anything about her or her kids.

"No one's in trouble," Leah said. "But this is Mister Shane's horse, and he wants to show you how to be safe around horses."

"Are you a real cowboy?" Dylan asked, pointing to Shane's hat.

Smiling, Shane took it off his head. "Why don't you come on over here and try it on?"

"Yeehaw!" Dylan ran toward him.

Ryan followed, but their sudden movements made the horse antsy. In a swift motion, Shane jumped between the horse and the boys, grabbing the horse by the halter. "Easy, Squirt."

The hat fluttered to the ground, and Ryan picked it up, then placed it on his head. "I cowboy. I ride horse."

Leah gathered him into her arms. "Not right now, you don't. This is Mister Shane's horse, and you have to ask him first."

And from the disapproving glare Shane was giving her, it wasn't likely to happen anytime soon.

"He said I could wear that hat," Dylan said, snatching the hat from his brother.

"Mine."

"But he said it was for me." As he adjusted the hat on his head, Dylan ran toward Shane and the horse. The horse whinnied, then started to dance around.

Shane brought his attention to Dylan. "Slow down, buddy. You scare the horse when you run."

Dylan stopped. He turned and stuck his tongue out at his brother, then looked at Shane. "Can we ride your horse, Mister Shane?"

"Not right now," Shane said. "Everyone who rides a horse has to know the safety rules first."

Even Leah knew that it wasn't safe for a child without any riding experience to be on a horse. But at least the man didn't make a promise he couldn't keep. When they had come here that summer, so long ago, Helen hadn't allowed Nicole to ride, except with an adult sitting in the saddle with her. She couldn't imagine that this man would be any different. In fact, judging by the way he continued to glower at her, he'd be even worse.

Nicole and Erin had come around the house. Erin waved, and Leah returned the gesture. At least they knew the boys were safe. Nicole went back into the house. Erin came toward them. When Leah turned her attention back to the boys, Shane had lifted Ryan up and was allowing him to pet the horse. At least he seemed nicer now. Leah had forgotten how the so-called real cowboys were more overprotective of their horses than she was of her sons.

"At least there's no traffic here for them to play in," Erin said, shaking her head.

Shane turned and looked at them. "Only a fool would think that there still aren't a lot of dangers to children here. There are coyotes, snakes—and those are just the common things to watch out for. And then there's something like my horse. You need to tell your kids that they can't come up to a strange animal like that. Squirt is easygoing enough. But if it had been one of my other mounts, you might not have been so fortunate."

"Well, aren't you a ray of sunshine?" Erin said. "They're small children, and we barely just got here. You can't expect them to show up and know everything all at once. Obviously, you haven't been around children much."

At the look Shane gave Erin, Leah grabbed her sister's arm. "It's fine. No harm was done, and when we get back to the house, we'll sit with the boys and lay down some ground rules."

"But I want to ride the horse," Dylan said, a stubborn expression filling his face. Leah knew that expression. Telling him no meant a tantrum would follow. And the last thing she needed was for her son to fall apart in front of this already-judgmental man.

"I believe Mister Shane said that you needed to learn the rules first. So, let's go inside and have a little snack, then we can talk."

The boys hadn't had lunch, either, which would make them crankier and more prone to difficulty if Leah didn't deal with it soon. They'd been sleeping, and she hadn't wanted to disturb them. Not something she would want to share with Mr. Judgy Pants. The boys hadn't been sleeping well lately with all the changes in their lives, and she had wanted to give them a break.

Unfortunately, her answer didn't sit well with Dylan. "I want to ride the horse now."

Shane set Ryan on the ground away from the horse and pointed him toward Leah. "Go see your momma."

At least Ryan did what he was told. Leah held her arms out to her son. "Are you ready for a snack?"

"I no have no lunch," he said, whining at the end.

"We can have sandwiches," she hugged him, enjoying the feeling of having her son back safely in her arms. Even though she already knew he was safe, holding him made it real.

"I hate sandwiches," Dylan said.

"I'm sure we can find something else that's tasty. Let's go see what's in the kitchen." Leah held out her hand, hoping that her son would take it.

But Dylan was still focused on the horse. "I want to ride the horse."

She took a step in his direction. She could feel Shane's eyes on her like he wasn't sure what she was going to do and wouldn't approve. He'd approved of nothing she'd done so far.

"We've already had this discussion. You need to come with me, so we can all have something to eat."

"No." Dylan crossed his arms over his chest, and Leah braced herself for what was coming.

The psychologist had told her it was a gift to see the signs of a tantrum forming, but right now, it felt like a burden. Especially with her little boy clinging to her and Shane's disapproving glare. Leah turned to her sister.

"Can you take Ryan inside for me? Dylan and I will be there shortly."

Erin nodded. She'd been her rock these past few months. At first, Leah had felt guilty relying so heavily on her sister when Erin was dealing with a tragedy of her own. Erin's daughter, Lily, had died in a tragic accident, and her marriage had ended as a result. But Erin had told her that helping with the boys was healing for her, and now Leah had no idea what she would have done without her.

"Come on, Ry-guy. Let's go eat and then we can figure out which room is yours."

Ryan eagerly went over to his aunt. He loved his Auntie Erin, and he was the sunshine to Dylan's thunderstorms. Once he and Erin had started toward the house, Leah turned her attention back to Dylan.

"You had your chance to do the right thing," she said. "Come now, or there will be consequences."

She already knew how this was going to end. But it was important to make Dylan aware that he was making a choice. Dylan picked up a rock.

"I told you I want to ride the horse." He turned and threw the rock at the horse, narrowly missing it.

"That's enough," Leah said, closing the distance between her and Dylan and taking him by the arm. "We do not throw rocks. And we especially don't throw them at another living being. You tell Mister Shane you're sorry."

"No." Dylan wrestled himself from her grasp, which hadn't been that tight, and threw himself to the ground. "I want to ride the horse."

He started wailing, kicking and screaming. This

would go on for a while, and there was nothing to do but let him finish it out.

Leah took a step back and turned to Shane. "I'm sorry my boys scared your horse. You'd best take him and be on your way. It'll be easier if the horse isn't here to distract him."

Shane shook his head slowly. "What are you going to do to him?"

"Nothing. He's going to sit here and throw his fit, and then we'll go back to the house and have something to eat."

"You said something about consequences. What are they?"

She knew the look on his face. It was the same one she got whenever Dylan threw a fit in public. Shane sounded like he thought she was going to beat him or something. But neither Shane nor the people who thought they could insert themselves into her business had spent countless hours in therapy with her son.

"He'll lose some of his privileges, including screen time. He and his brother had too much of it on the drive anyway. I'm sure that's why he's acting up now."

Shane looked doubtful. "I'd like to check on him later."

Who was this man to think he knew everything there was to know about her family?

"What do you think, little guy? Can I come see you later?" Shane bent in front of Dylan only to get a handful of dirt tossed in his face.

"Hey!" Shane jumped and wiped at his eyes. She probably should have warned him not to go near her son while he was in the middle of a fit. For a seven-year-old, Dylan could be incredibly violent. But it wasn't his fault. The past few years had been chaotic for him, and he was acting out of the fear and insecurity planted in him by his unstable father. Jason was a great dad when he was clean, but his relapses turned their lives upside down. Things had gotten worse since Jason's death from a drug overdose. In a child's mind, a terrible father was better than a dead father.

"Please ignore him," she said, motioning for Shane to come near her.

Wiping the dust from his face, Shane sputtered as he walked in her direction. "He just threw dirt in my face."

"Maybe you should have waited for my response before stepping in. Right now, he is so deep in his animal instincts that he can't be rational or reasoned with. As I said, you should go now. I'm going to sit here and wait this out."

It was exhausting enough having to deal with Dylan's fit. But having to once again justify her actions made Leah even wearier. She'd hoped that coming out to this isolated ranch with her sisters, who also understood how to handle Dylan, would allow her to get a break from the judgment of everyone around her.

To help Shane see her resolve, Leah sat on a nearby rock. But instead of doing as she asked, Shane came and sat next to her.

So much for getting a break.

The last thing Shane needed was to get involved with a single mother desperately in need of a daddy figure for her children. Been there, done that and even had a World's Greatest Dad coffee mug to show for it. But when Gina had ridden out of town on the back of a

Harley with a guy who promised more excitement than he could, she'd taken Natalie, and there hadn't been a single thing to do about it. Unless a man legally adopted a child, he had no rights to the kid in the future.

And yet, there was something about Leah and the pain written on her face that drew him. She might not want him here, but he couldn't bring himself to leave.

When Helen was alive, she'd told him about her exhusband, the Colonel, and how her biggest regret in divorcing him had been leaving his three daughters behind. She'd loved them like her own, but she'd been given no visitation rights. However, she'd continued to pray for the girls every single day. When Gina left, Helen had been his rock. She'd told him about her love for the girls, and while he had been comforted by the fact that he wasn't alone in his pain, he also wasn't ready to befriend a beautiful woman with two kids he'd never have any right to.

Except he'd promised Helen he'd look out for the girls. Only they weren't girls now but grown women, and keeping his promise wasn't looking as easy as it had been to make it. Still, Helen had been there for him in his darkest days. In many ways, she'd been like a mother to him. He owed it to her to be there for the girls she'd been unable to love the way she'd have liked.

Dylan continued to scream and flail in the dirt. Shane had moved Squirt to a safer spot where the little boy wouldn't be tempted by him and Squirt wouldn't be spooked. Leah said she had everything under control. But, from Shane's perspective, this was a mess. How could she let her son act like this?

Worse, he couldn't believe she'd gotten into this mess in the first place. Though he was in no position to judge, it seemed like poor parenting to leave your children alone like she had. He'd often watched Natalie for Gina because otherwise Gina would have left Natalie alone. Once again, he wondered exactly how much his promise to Helen was going to cost him.

He glanced over at Leah, trying to gauge her reaction. She sat there, acting like she didn't have a care in the world, picking several of the long blades of grass that had gone far too long without cutting. She was twisting them into some kind of shape.

"What are you making?" he asked.

A soft smile crossed her face. "I was trying to remember how to make the little grass baskets Helen had taught us to make when we were small. I thought it would be fun to teach the boys."

She held it up, then frowned slightly. "I'm missing a step. I wonder if I can look it up online to find the answer."

"I've never done anything like that," Shane said. "All I know how to do with grass is make a whistle."

He picked a few blades, then demonstrated.

At the sound, Leah smiled. "Oh, that's wonderful. You'll have to show me how to do it. The boys will think it's so fun."

At her words, Dylan paused and looked over at them. Leah shot Shane a look.

"Show me," she said, her eyes darting to Dylan before she shook her head at Shane. She seemed to be signaling him to continue ignoring Dylan.

Even though it didn't seem right to not acknowledge the boy's silence, Shane did as she asked. Leah picked some grass of her own and tried copying his motion, but all she accomplished was contorting her face and sending the grass flying through the air.

Dylan giggled.

Leah didn't look at him and instead tried again.

As she had in her previous attempt, she failed.

"You need to roll your tongue slightly," Shane said. "I can't tell if you're doing it or not, but when my dad taught me how to whistle, that's what he told me to do."

Once more, Leah took some grass and tried to make it whistle.

Dylan got up and came over to them. "You're doing it wrong. Let me show you."

He tried taking the grass out of her hand, but she shook her head. "I'm done. Let's go inside and have some lunch."

For a moment, Dylan looked like he was going to argue, but then he nodded. "I'm hungry."

"All right then."

Leah got up and brushed the dirt from her pants. She smiled at Shane. "As you can see, everything is okay now. We're going to go inside and eat. You should take your horse home."

Once again, she was dismissing him. And it still didn't feel right.

"We should talk about what just happened," he said. Talking wasn't his strong suit, but the situation had been intense. He'd come by to be neighborly and had ended up in the middle of a family crisis.

Dylan had already started for the house. She turned and gave Shane the kind of stern look he imagined she used on her sons.

"There's nothing to talk about. I have everything

perfectly in hand. You don't need to feel obligated to look out for my children or me. We'll be fine."

The resignation in her voice told him that there was a lot more to her story then he knew. Sure, he knew the little Helen had told him over the years. But she hadn't been in contact with the girls enough to have details beyond the newspaper clippings of marriage and death announcements she collected. There were also a couple of articles about a man being found dead of a drug overdose, the death of a little girl, and one about a fatal car accident. The bare bones, not enough to know anything other than these women had been through a lot recently. Leah's husband had died weeks before Helen passed. Was that why her parenting seemed so chaotic?

Maybe sticking around to see what he could do to help wouldn't hurt.

"We're neighbors. Helen was a good friend. She wanted me to look out for you."

Leah shook her head. "Look, I know you think I'm a terrible mom. But you have no idea what we've been through, and we're doing our best to move on."

She gestured at the house, and one of the sisters was beckoning Dylan inside.

"Since things got bad with his dad, we've been in therapy. I worked two jobs to pay for a child psychologist to help us figure out how to handle these fits. As for your horse, I know things got out of hand. I'm sorry for that. In the future, please don't bring him over."

Though she still sounded weary, there was a determined expression on her face that made him realize she was stronger than he had first thought.

"I just want to help," he said.

"Then go home. I don't know what Helen told you about our childhood or what you've read in the papers about us. But if you think that any of it means we need someone to take care of us, you're wrong. We've learned how to take care of ourselves. We don't need you."

It was as if she had read his earlier thoughts. The stubborn set to her jaw and the pain in her eyes made him want to take care of her anyway. But he also knew that it wasn't worth the grief it would bring to his own life to chase after a woman who didn't want him.

So how was he supposed to keep his promise to Helen?

"Okay." He reached into his pocket and pulled out a business card for his ranch. He'd bought a hundred of them years ago and still had more than he could count left. At least he'd be getting rid of one more. "My number's on here. You might not need me now, but if there's anything I can do to help you all get settled, give me a call."

She took the card, but from the look on her face, it would probably go straight into the round file when she got inside. "Thanks."

He watched as she walked into her house, her posture straight and determined, and yet the air of sadness around her made him wish he could do more for her. But that was the kind of thinking that got a man in trouble. How many times had he tried playing the white knight, saving the damsel in distress? And while he'd been taken advantage of in the past, Leah was different. She didn't want anything to do with him.

Chapter Two

Shane didn't need anything from the sale barn, but he stopped by the Wednesday livestock auction just the same. It was a good chance to socialize with the other ranchers in the area and to keep up on the news. Most folks wouldn't call Columbine Springs a happening place, but if you wanted to know what was happening, at least among the ranchers, the sale barn was where you'd find out.

"Hey, Shane!" Arnold Hastings, one of the old-timers, gave him a wave. "We were just talking about that bull of yours. Ol' Mike was wanting to add a new bloodline to his herd. I told him that you won't find a finer bull than Big Red."

Given that Arnold had his own prize-winning bull, it was a fine compliment. "Thank you. I appreciate it. Do they have anything good for sale today?"

Arnold shook his head as he chewed on a piece of hay. "Nope. Bobby's trying to get rid of that old mare of his again, but he can't seem to get it through his thick skull that no one wants that useless mare. 'Bout all she's good for is being led around on a rope. Even then, the creature is better off being put out to pasture. But since Bobby's little girl won a bunch of buckles on her barrel racing, he's sure someone's going to be willing to pay a lot of money for her."

An image of the little boys next door came to mind. Shane hadn't been back since he met them last week. He'd wanted to give them time, but he also wasn't sure how to approach them since Leah had made it clear she didn't want him there.

He'd promised the boys he'd teach them the rules about horses, and then they could ride. But none of his mounts were suitable for children, especially the little one. Natalie had taken her horse when she and Gina had left.

"There's nothing wrong with my horse," Bobby said, joining the conversation. "Belle is a great mare, and she'd be perfect for someone with kids. She won a lot of buckles for my Sara."

Just then, a lightbulb went off. The problem was, Leah didn't want him butting into her life. But if she did warm up to the idea of having him around for the sake of the boys...

"How much do you want for her?" Shane asked.

Bobby grinned. "I told Frank I wouldn't take less than five grand. But for you, I'd take two and a half."

Was he seriously considering spending twenty-five hundred dollars on a horse for a couple of kids he wasn't even sure would get to ride it?

He hesitated.

"Now, Shane, that's a good deal, and you know it."

Arnold snorted. "You just offered that mare to Jimmy Ball for two grand last week."

"And he's real interested, so you better make it quick."

The last thing he needed was another animal to feed. Not with things so uncertain now that he wasn't sure if the women would let him graze his cattle at Helen's ranch. He'd intended to ask them, but as firm as Leah had been in sending him away, he was having his lawyer draw up an agreement, so everything was in writing. He and Helen hadn't needed one, but the women seemed like they would want it.

"I'm not interested," Shane said. "I was just curious what you were asking, in case I run into someone in need of a retired barrel-racing horse."

At the word *retired*, Arnold snickered. Bobby glared at him and started to speak, but before Shane could figure out what he was saying, a familiar voice rang out.

"I'm here to buy some cows."

Leah.

At least now he knew they intended to work the land themselves, so they probably wouldn't be interested in leasing him the land for grazing. Good thing he hadn't jumped on the horse offer, since now he'd be figuring out a new financial plan.

"I ain't seen her around before," Bobby said. "Look at that. There's two of 'em."

Three, actually, but Shane wasn't going to correct him.

Arnold got out of his chair. "I wonder if those are the girls who inherited the old Wanamaker place. Helen was making noises about leaving it to her ex's kids. Don't know why. It's not like they're family or anything. I figured they'd probably sell the place and move on."

As Arnold chattered on about what he thought of the situation, Shane walked over to Leah.

"Nice to see you again," he said, approaching her.

"Likewise." She didn't sound like she meant it. "I believe you know my sister Erin."

Shane tipped his hat to her. "Ma'am." Then he looked around. "Where are the boys?"

Leah gave him the same irritated look she'd given him when he'd asked her questions the day they'd met. Maybe she just looked irritated all the time. Which would be a shame because, other than the angry lines on her face, she was downright pretty. Dark brown hair, brown eyes, pink lips…what was he doing?

"They're not lost, if that's what you're implying," Leah said. "They're home with our sister Nicole, who has a degree in early childhood education."

Great. He was trying to be polite, and she took it as an insult. "I didn't mean anything by it. I was asking after them, so I could say hi."

Erin leaned in to say something to Leah, who nodded. Leah turned her attention back to him. "I'm sorry. I misunderstood. I'm a little sensitive where my kids are concerned."

A little? Shane was tempted to say something, but Leah already looked like she was hankering for a fight.

"No harm done," Shane said instead. "What brings you to the sale barn today? I heard you asking about cows. I have a herd of my own. I could help if you want."

Most people didn't look like they wanted to bite his head off when he was trying to be neighborly. Maybe his original theory of Leah always looking cranky wasn't too far off the mark.

"We're going to turn it back into a working ranch," Erin said, sounding way more cheerful than her sister. "We've decided to call it Three Sisters Ranch, and it's our fresh start. I've been studying brands, and I think I've come up with the perfect one. So now, all we need are some cows."

And a lick of common sense. But at least Erin seemed excited about the plan. Whereas Leah...

Leah just looked weary. Like the last place on earth she wanted to be was at the sale barn, picking out cows for their new ranch adventure. Did they have any idea what they were getting into?

"How many cows are you thinking of getting?"

Maybe the best way to handle the situation was to ask them questions so that they would realize that there was more to ranching than buying cows.

Erin's face lit up. She was pretty, too, but not in the same way as Leah. Erin naturally seemed like the sort to smile a lot and be happy, which should have made her more attractive. But it was Leah who drew him. Of course he would be attracted to the difficult one. Why make it easy on himself?

"Oh, I don't know," Erin said. "I'd like some of those cute black-and-white ones, and Nicole wants us to see if we can find some Highland cows. She fell in love with them when she went to Scotland, and now that we have a ranch, we're going to get her some."

How did you explain to someone that their idea was completely crazy when they were so clearly excited?

"You know the cute black-and-white ones are dairy cows, right?"

He hoped he didn't sound too condescending, because that was sure to set Leah off. But the ranch wasn't set up for a dairy operation. If they bought dairy cows, they'd be throwing their money away.

"We don't know anything about cows," Leah said slowly. Then she muttered, "I knew this was too good to be true."

Erin nudged her. "Stop being the little black rain cloud. That's what the internet is for. We've also got books in Helen's library. She must've owned every book ever written about ranching."

He hadn't expected the lump that formed in his throat at her words. Helen had loved books, and in the early days of his ranch, she'd often lent him the ones she thought he'd find most helpful. Before she'd passed, she'd given him a few of her most treasured books.

"She did love her books," Shane said, hoping they didn't hear the catch in his voice. "She gave me a few of her favorites when she got sick, if you'd like to look at them."

At the mention of Helen, the women exchanged another set of looks, communicating something he couldn't understand, yet, for some reason, he wanted to.

"I didn't realize she was sick," Leah said quietly. "We didn't know much about her later years, and it feels weird to be given such a gift when we weren't close. Thank you for being there to take care of her."

The obvious sympathy in her voice softened his heart. Perhaps he'd been too hasty in dismissing her as cranky. There was a gentleness in her eyes that seemed to peek out from the wariness at unexpected moments.

Erin linked arms with her sister. "Yes, thank you.

We have good memories of her, and we hated not being in better touch. But with things being the way they were, it wasn't possible."

He'd heard enough stories about the Colonel to know that with the way he ruled the family, even if the girls had tried to stay in touch, he wouldn't have allowed it. At the sadness in their voices, he couldn't help wondering if they felt the same deep sense of loss when their father and Helen had divorced.

Maybe there was more to Leah's attitude than he could see. If it had been any other woman, he'd have declared her as having too much baggage and run the other way. But remembering the sadness on Helen's face as she talked about her poor girls, he knew he had no choice but to see it through.

"Water under the bridge," he said. "Helen understood your situation, and I never heard her speak anything but love toward you all. That's why she asked me to look after you and help out if you needed it."

Too bad he hadn't done a good job of it so far. Helen would have boxed his ears for sure if she'd been capable of such things. He'd let Leah's anger keep him away when he should have been trying harder to help them.

"We do appreciate the advice you've given us. I guess we have a little more reading to do before we buy any livestock," Leah said, starting to turn away.

Erin let out a long sigh as she followed her sister. "We have to start turning a profit soon," she muttered.

"We'll figure it out." He could hear Leah's words as they walked over to sign up for the auction.

She might be willing to figure it out, but they were going to be in for a world of hurt if they were so ignorant as to walk into a sale barn, hoping to buy cows based on how cute they were.

He jogged to catch up with them. "Let me help you. A lot of the cows they have here today aren't worth buying, and I'm familiar with all the local ranchers. They don't mean to cheat anyone, but they would have no problem taking money from someone who doesn't know any better."

The sisters exchanged a look, then Leah nodded. "We don't have a lot of money to waste, so we appreciate the help."

It seemed a hard-won agreement, but he was glad that she could at least see sense. He recognized that wary expression in her eyes again, and it struck him harder than he'd expected. Though Helen had told him about the girls' rough childhood, he also hadn't expected to see how it had impacted them as adults. To have it impact him. He'd grown up in a different but equally unstable situation. That kind of life where you're afraid to trust or lean on anyone too much, because you know they'll be gone soon, and you'll be stuck on your own, trying to figure things out.

No wonder the sisters were so quick to shove him aside and not want his help. They wanted to do it on their own because they figured that, at some point, he'd be gone and they'd have to rely on themselves again.

So how could he show them that he wasn't going anywhere?

More important, how could he be there for them without ending up the fool, running around taking care of them, only to be dropped when a bigger, better deal came through?

These women needed rescuing. He liked to be the hero. But he was tired of being taken advantage of and abandoned when he wasn't needed anymore.

Still, he gave a nod as he led them deeper into the sale barn.

There wasn't a single cow to be had. At least none worth buying, according to Shane. Even though Leah hated being so reliant on him, as he patiently explained to her what he was looking at as he examined each cow, she was glad for his expert opinion. He'd even stopped Leah from buying the pretty chicken, which had turned out to be a rooster, so it would have also been useless to them.

What was the point in inheriting a ranch when you couldn't do anything with it? Helen had leased out the land, but it was for such a small sum, Leah and her sisters wouldn't have enough money to live off of. According to Helen's old records, the ranch had once been a thriving business. Surely, it could be successful once again.

Yes, they now had a place to live, and with Leah's financial situation, it was a real blessing. Erin hadn't gotten any money out of her divorce, since her ex wanted to keep the house, and it was worth less than what they'd paid for it when they'd bought it. She'd considered herself lucky to have been able to walk away. Nicole had never made a lot as a preschool teacher, so she didn't have much money, either. Needless to say, the sisters needed some way to make money to keep food in their stomachs and the lights on. They'd gotten a ranch, yes, but the attorney had very apologetically told the women that Helen didn't leave much in the way of cash.

So how were they supposed to make money? Based on the budget they'd come up with, they had about six months to figure it out.

"Let me buy you ladies a cup of coffee," Shane said, indicating a café down the street. "I know you must be disappointed to not find any cows, but it's the wrong time of year, and I'd hate for you to be stuck with something that would be a financial burden."

The last thing she wanted to do was sit and have coffee when she had plans to make. But he hadn't been anything but nice to them, and it would be rude to refuse. It was a small town, and she couldn't afford to alienate anyone, even though all she wanted was to be left alone.

"That would be great, thank you." Leah smiled at him, then looked over at her sister. "You don't mind, do you?"

"Of course not. Though we should probably be doing the buying, considering he probably saved us thousands of dollars."

Erin had a point, but Shane shook his head.

"A gentleman would never let the lady buy. Besides, it's only a couple of cups of coffee. Though Della makes the best bear claws, and you should probably have one. I know I'm going to." His grin warmed her. When he wasn't looking at her like he thought she was the world's worst mother or the biggest ignoramus to show up in town, he seemed almost…nice.

The lawyer did confirm that Shane had been a big help to Helen. Maybe, if they all got to know one another, they could be friends. Or at least friendly. It wouldn't hurt to have a neighbor to call on in case of emergency. Not that she had any plans of relying on him, since she'd already promised herself never to depend on a man again.

"Then we must insist upon having you over for dinner sometime. Nicole has been bugging me to make my famous lasagna, so set a date, and we'll have it."

As he held the door open to the café, Shane gave her another encouraging smile. "Now that's an offer I can't refuse. I cook well enough that I don't starve to death, but it's been a long time since I've had homemade lasagna."

"Leah's is the best. I can't tell you how many times I had her over at my house, trying to teach me. But mine was never as good. I'm sure she must put in some secret ingredient when my back is turned, but she's always denied it."

Leah laughed. "I promise I've always shown you exactly the way I do it. Maybe the difference is love. I could spend all day in the kitchen and be perfectly happy, whereas you spend so much time complaining and fussing that I'm sure it makes your food bitter."

"Maybe," Erin said. "But I still think you're holding out on me."

Smiling at their old argument, Leah felt Shane's eyes on her. Erin had always been the pretty one, so why didn't he focus on her instead? Was that why he was being so friendly? Because he saw Leah as a potential date? She was so not interested. A younger version of herself might have been, but she knew better now.

Though she sometimes questioned why Helen never

remarried, Leah could understand how being burned would leave a person wary. Leah wasn't sure she'd ever be able to trust a man again, let alone fall in love.

Inside the café, an older woman greeted them warmly. "Shane! Are these your sisters? I'm so glad to see that you finally have family visiting."

Shane looked at them and shrugged, then shook his head. "No. They're the ones who inherited Helen's ranch. I'm helping them get settled. We'd like three coffees and bear claws, if you have any left."

He hadn't actually asked them if they wanted bear claws, but as Della lifted the domed lid off the tray, Leah wasn't going to complain. It had been forever since she'd indulged in any kind of pastry because of how she limited the sugar her boys consumed. It didn't seem fair to have treats for herself and deny them.

"It's nice to meet you," Della said as she put bear claws on plates. "I hope you'll be sticking around Columbine Springs. I always hate it when people turn our ranches into vacation homes that never get lived in."

Leah smiled. "My sisters and I plan on making this our home. I'm Leah, and this is my sister Erin. At home is my sister Nicole, and my two sons, Dylan and Ryan."

"Wonderful. So nice to have more families coming to our town. What about your husband?"

An innocent question but, as always, it was a knife to her gut. "He's dead."

"Oh, I'm so sorry for your loss. Forgive me for assuming."

The older woman looked so sad that Leah almost felt bad for having told her. "It's okay. The boys had to have come from somewhere, didn't they?"

She gave a small laugh, even though she didn't feel much like laughing.

"True," Della said. "Still, we're glad to have you here. I hope you'll be joining us at Faith Community Church on Sunday. Your family will find a warm welcome, and Pastor Jeff is a real man of God."

The Colonel had made them go to stuffy, oppressive churches that were all about following the rules and being obedient. Those churches had all given them warm welcomes when they first arrived, but the warmth was quickly replaced with disapproval over every sin they committed. What would this church think when they found out about the last years of her marriage? When they saw how Dylan acted up? When they heard about Erin's divorce or about Nicole's fiancé leaving her at the altar, only to be killed in a car accident with her maid of honor?

As much as people talked about the love of God, not one person who had claimed to be a Christian had reached out to their family in comfort. Instead, they were all quick to point out what the women had done wrong in their lives to have deserved such punishment from God.

But before Leah could come up with an appropriate excuse, Erin asked, "Is that the church Helen went to?"

Leah looked at her sister. The women in Erin's church had shunned her for her divorce. Why would she be so curious about this one?

"Yes. It was terrible when Helen got so sick, not having her there. Some of us would go to her house every Thursday for a Bible study, so she didn't feel like she was missing out. The church was never the same."

But Helen had been divorced. Why would this church be nice to her?

"I loved going to church with Helen when we were little," Erin said. "I know it sounds crazy, but I always felt a tangible love from God when I was there."

How Erin could still be open to going to church, Leah didn't know. But she couldn't begrudge her sister any happiness, not when Erin's life had been so difficult over the past year. It was odd that Erin had lost the most of all the sisters, a beloved child, yet she still managed to be the most cheerful. Not the fake cheer that Leah found herself mustering up every single day for her sons, but there was something deep down in Erin that found a way to be happy despite everything.

Some days, Leah wished she could find a little of that for herself.

"I hope you'll join us on Sunday," Della said with a smile. "I know it will be an answer to Helen's prayers."

"We'd be delighted," Erin answered for them both.

Leah had already told Erin that she had no intention of stepping inside a church ever again. But she wouldn't argue with her sister here. In fact, she didn't have the heart to argue with her at all. As usual, Leah would paste a smile on her face and do her best to make it through. At least until they kicked them out. Which they would, as soon as they met the boys.

Shane paid for their coffees and pastries and led them to an open table. Many of the other tables were full of men in cowboy hats talking over their own mugs of coffee. This was real ranch country, and it seemed so different after spending so many years in Denver.

"I know you had your hearts set on running the ranch. But Helen sold off the livestock and let things go into disrepair after her brother Norm died. She only kept a few chickens, and even the coop is no longer useable. It would take a lot of time and money to get everything back in working order."

Of course it would. The two things they had the least of were the most necessary.

"We need to make a living," Leah said.

Shane nodded. "When Helen was alive, she leased her land to me so I could run my cattle. It was enough for her to live on, though I suppose with more of you, it wouldn't stretch as far. Still, it's a fair amount of money and no work for you. I'd be happy to teach you what I know, and in the next year or so, you could decide if starting a ranch again would be worth the effort."

It sounded almost too good to be true. The lawyer had asked them what they were going to do about Shane's lease. This wasn't a pity offer, but something Shane needed as badly as they did. From what the lawyer said, if Shane couldn't graze on their land, he would have to buy hay, which was more expensive.

"What do we do about the shortfall?" Leah asked, looking at her sister. Leah had worked several jobs over the years, but it had been hard keeping them because her sons had been kicked out of too many day cares. That's why running the ranch had been such a good idea. They could all work from home, and they wouldn't need someone to watch the boys.

Not that the boys were Erin's problem. Or Nicole's. Which was why Leah hated the idea of having to find a job and asking her sisters to watch them.

"I could see if anyone needs an accountant," Erin

said. "I haven't worked in a while, but I've kept up my CPA license."

"If you're serious, I know several ranchers, myself included, who could use your help."

Erin smiled. "That would be great. I don't like to complain, but I would appreciate having the mental challenge again. Sometimes it's hard being alone with my own thoughts."

Strange how her sister could be so different. All Leah wanted was the chance to be alone for a while. But she supposed they both had their own ways of dealing with pain.

"Great. If you give me your information, I'll pass it around." If Leah wanted to accuse Shane of merely tossing them a bone to get them to agree to lease their land, it wasn't obvious by the look on his face.

Erin would tell her that she was being too cynical. And perhaps she was. But Leah had lost everything except her sons because of her blind faith in others.

As if he knew she wasn't quite ready to trust him, Shane turned his attention back to Leah. "Helen and I always operated by handshake agreement, but I'm sure you're expecting something more formal. My attorney is drawing up the papers for the lease. I'll bring it by when it's ready."

He was going out of his way to be fair. But Leah also couldn't bring herself to give him the same wide-eyed look her sister had. Perhaps the difference between Leah and Erin was that Leah's life had been destroyed by someone she trusted, whereas Erin's tragedy was simply one of those random terrible things that tears a person apart.

"That would be good, thanks," she said. "You can bring them when you come to dinner."

At least no one could accuse her of being inhospitable. But she hated the way he smiled at her, trying to make her like him. If she was honest with herself, there was probably a lot to like about Shane. But she'd been burned by too many smiles that said, "Trust me," and she wasn't willing to take a chance again.

Especially because she could feel tiny flutters of… No. She wasn't going there.

To take her mind off the uneasy feeling in her stomach, she took a bite of the bear claw. It was every bit as good as she'd hoped. She looked around the small café, watching these cowboys, who were probably her neighbors, interact. Why couldn't Shane be one of those older men with the handlebar moustaches that were so completely unattractive that she wouldn't have a problem looking at him?

Fortunately, Erin started grilling him about the area, which took Shane's attention off Leah. At least mostly. He still kept stealing glances at her like he was trying to figure her out or gauge her reactions. Like he cared about what she thought.

But that was one more distraction she didn't want, either. All she wanted was to establish a new life for herself and her sons with her sisters. There was no room in her life for some cowboy.

She drained the rest of her coffee, then looked at her sister. "We should get back. The boys probably have Nicole tied up by now. And we should discuss what's next with her."

Erin nodded. "You're right. We've tossed out ideas, but it's not fair to not include her. I know she was really in love with the idea of having some Highland cows. And chickens."

"And horses and goats," Leah said, grinning. Nicole had been the most excited about having a ranch. She might hate the idea of leasing the land and not making a go of things on their own.

Shane stood and gathered their trash. "You can still have animals. I'd be happy to help repair the chicken coop. It shouldn't take much since Helen had chickens up until about a year ago."

There he went again, being helpful.

"Yes, it will," Erin said. "And while we appreciate all your offers, we don't want to take advantage. You'd be surprised at how capable we are of taking care of ourselves. Leah has already done a lot of work on the ranch. You wouldn't believe how good she is with a set of tools. It's amazing how much the three of us can do when we work together."

At least Leah wasn't alone in wanting to do as much as they could on their own. The women had discussed their frustration at feeling helpless at the end of their respective relationships. It was good for them to do things for themselves.

Shane nodded like he understood. "I'm always happy to lend a hand. That's what neighbors do."

Neighbors. Leah's had all pretty much abandoned her when Jason had begun his downward spiral. Her sisters hadn't seemed to have had any to speak of, at least none who'd befriended them. Helen used to talk about being neighborly, and Leah vaguely remembered barbecues and picnics. But she wasn't sure how to translate that all into her life now.

She wanted to believe the expression of kindness on

his face, but where would trusting him get her? She'd been hurt and heartbroken too many times already. Holding out hope for someone who was probably only going to let her down was a waste of effort. Leah had her sisters and her sons, and that was enough.

It had to be.

Chapter Three

Though the invitation had been friendly enough when it had been issued, Shane couldn't help feeling unwanted when he arrived for dinner later that week. It wasn't that they had put out a mat in front of the door that said Go Away, but they might as well have.

Leah ushered him into the kitchen with a frown so deep, it almost made him wonder if someone had died. But since all his previous attempts at humor had gone astray with her, he wasn't going to mention it. The house was quiet, and while he would have liked to have asked about the boys, that also hadn't gone well the last time. Usually, he got along with everyone. But for whatever reason, he couldn't connect with Leah.

"Is there anything I can do to help?" he asked, hoping he sounded friendly and nonthreatening.

With most people, he'd have given up by now. But he couldn't forget the sadness in Helen's voice whenever she'd talked about her girls and the difficulties they'd had in life. He wanted to think that whatever kept them so closed off was more about the tragedies they had suffered than anything he had done. But maybe it was a good place to start a conversation.

When the shake of her head was accompanied by yet another scowl, he knew he couldn't let it go.

"Have I done something to offend you?"

She stopped, holding the pitcher she'd just brought over to the sink. "No. Why do you ask?"

"You seem distant. Like you don't want me here. You've barely said a word to me, and everything I can think of saying to you, I'm afraid it will only make the distance greater."

Leah looked genuinely wounded by his words. Like he'd called her out in a harsher way than he'd intended.

"I'm sorry," she said, setting the pitcher on the counter and wiping her hands on her apron. "It's been a rough day. Erin is interviewing at a nearby ranch to do their books, and Nicole ran to the store for more bread. The boys are asleep on the couch, and when you got here, I was focused on being quiet so they wouldn't wake up."

He followed her gaze as she looked around the kitchen and realized that the room was in shambles. "I'd hoped to have everything cleaned up before you got here, but time got away from me."

She gave a small shrug, then pointed at the oven. "But at least dinner is cooking, and that part I know will be all right. If you can bear with me, I promise it will get better."

A small cry came from the other room. Leah rubbed her head. "I'd hoped they would sleep a little longer, so I could get things cleaned up."

Shane felt guilty for having judged her. Now that

he was really looking at her, he could see the signs of an exhausted mother trying to do her best.

"I've already gathered that you don't like accepting help, but please, tell me something I can do to make it easier for you until your sisters get here."

Ryan walked in, wearing a shirt and nothing else, carrying a diaper. "I all wet," he said.

"Let me help you, buddy. Can you show me where your mom keeps your diapers?"

Leah looked like she was going to argue, but Shane shook his head. "I've changed a diaper or two in my lifetime. I've got this. You finish doing what you need to get dinner ready. I'll keep the boys occupied."

He could see her hesitation, but then Ryan pointed at his cowboy hat. "I wear hat?"

Her resigned sigh felt less like a victory than he'd wanted, but at least she nodded. "Thanks."

"Let's get you in some clean, dry pants, and then we'll see about fixing you up with my hat." Shane held his hand out to the little boy, who grinned.

"I be cowboy!"

As he took Ryan's hand, he could see the tension ease from Leah's face. It was hard to tell what was going on in her mind, but at least she seemed more relaxed. She turned back to the sink, and the little boy led him out of the room.

They walked down the hall to the bedroom Helen had used when she had gotten sick. The hospital bed had been taken out, and two twin beds neatly made with denim-looking bedspreads dominated the room. Ryan pointed to a dresser that had a stack of diapers and wipes on top of it.

Though it had been a while since Shane had changed

a diaper, he managed to get the little boy situated quickly. When they were finished, Ryan pointed to Shane's hat.

"I wear hat now?"

Shane took off his hat and placed it on the little boy's head. "Here you go, partner."

"I ride da horse?"

"I didn't bring him today."

His face scrunched up, and with a pang, Shane remembered the fit his brother had thrown. Was he in for the same with this little guy? Ordinarily, Shane would feel confident in his ability to handle it. But considering how nervous Leah had seemed at letting him watch her son, he didn't want to mess it up.

It was a mistake, getting so emotionally involved with this family. He shouldn't care so much about Leah, but he knew that telling himself he was just being neighborly was a lie. He was an idiot, wanting to fix a woman who was so obviously broken. Why couldn't he be attracted to the ones who didn't seem to need him?

Shane squatted down in front of Ryan. "How about we play horses instead?"

"How do you do that?" Dylan stood in the doorway, the same suspicious look his mother often wore upon his face.

At least he knew the child came by it honestly.

"You've never played horses?"

Dylan crossed his arms over his chest. "Maybe. How do you play it?"

Shane got on his hands and knees. "Like this. We all pretend to be horses."

He looked over at Ryan. "What does a horse say?"

"Neigh!" A wide grin split his face as he made the sound. Ryan also got on his hands and knees and started crawling around the floor. "Neigh," he said again.

Shane looked over at Dylan. "Are you going to join us?"

"What if I want to ride the horse?"

If it had just been Ryan, Shane would have gladly agreed. But with the way he'd seen the boys fight before, he wasn't sure he wanted to open that can of worms. And yet, the way Ryan looked at him, he didn't have the heart to say no.

"You and your brother have to take turns." He sat up and pulled his phone out of his pocket. "I'm going to set the alarm for five minutes. You can ride on my back until it rings. Then it's Ryan's turn."

"Can I wear your hat, like a real cowboy?"

He looked over at Ryan, who was still wearing his hat. "I already said Ryan could wear it. So you'll have to ask him."

Dylan reached for the hat, but Shane put his hand out. "You can't just take it. You have to ask."

"Can I have a turn please?"

Ryan smiled and took off the hat. "I be horse. You be cowboy."

And just like that, Dylan put the cowboy hat on his head, then climbed on Shane's back. They pranced around the room like horses, and Dylan was surprisingly gentle. Maybe what he had experienced before had just been a bad day. The way the boys played and cooperated with him, it brought back pangs of regret at how things had ended between him and Gina. Helen had always told him that he could meet someone else and have children with her, but the options for meeting young, marriageable women in Columbine Springs were next to zero. He'd been lucky to have found Gina.

He liked to think he would have made a great father.

But as much as these boys reminded him of that dream, this time he wouldn't get attached. He wasn't going to let himself fall in love with a couple of kids that couldn't be his. And he certainly wasn't going to let whatever misguided feelings he had for their mother make himself want something he could never have.

Watching Shane play with her sons brought tears to Leah's eyes. She couldn't remember ever seeing Jason do that with them. Maybe Dylan, when he was small. But so much of their trouble began when she was pregnant with Ryan that the boy had never really bonded with his father. She liked how Shane got on the ground with them and played.

A sound behind her made Leah turn.

"He's good with them, isn't he?" Nicole asked. "There's nothing more heartwarming than seeing a man interact with children like this."

Leah smiled at her sister. "Yes. But don't go planning any weddings. I know how that mind of yours works."

"I wouldn't dream of it. That was the old Nicole. Until recently, I believed in happily ever after, and I thought I was doing everyone a favor by shipping them. But now I have to wonder, who is it possible for? None of us seem to have figured it out, and I found out that another one of my friends is getting divorced. I don't think forever means what any of us think it means."

Leah put her arm around Nicole and gave her a quick hug. Out of the three sisters, Nicole had always been the optimist. But that optimism had been replaced by a deep cynicism that made Leah want to cry. At least Erin had enough optimism for them all. How her sister managed to find happiness after so much heartbreak, Leah didn't know. But at least they all had each other. One of the therapists had asked Leah about her resiliency, and Leah had told her quite honestly that she wouldn't have been able to make it without her sisters. She only hoped that she was doing the same for them.

"Thanks," Nicole said. "I don't mean to be such a downer, but Fernando called again today. It drives me crazy that he keeps thinking he needs to check on me and make sure I'm okay. He's not the one who ran off with my fiancé on my wedding day. I wish he would leave me alone instead of constantly calling and trying to make it up to me."

This was one subject Leah knew better than to disagree with her sister on. Fernando Montoya's sister, Adriana, had been Nicole's best friend. At least until Adriana had run off with Nicole's fiancé, Brandon, leaving Nicole at the altar. Unfortunately, Adriana and Brandon were killed in a car accident before Nicole could confront them. Apparently, Fernando had known about the affair and felt guilty he hadn't done more to stop it. With Adriana and Brandon gone, Fernando liked to check in with Nicole regularly to make sure she was doing okay.

Maybe they all were a bunch of curmudgeons who couldn't accept help from anyone else. Though Leah thought Fernando's concern was sweet, she could also understand why her sister wanted him to leave her alone.

They'd all been hurt too much by the people who were supposed to be there for them. It was too exhausting to keep believing in anyone outside their circle.

"I'm sorry he's still bothering you. It's probably his way of dealing with his grief. It just stinks that he has to keep dragging you through it." She hoped her words sounded helpful and not condescending. After all, it wasn't like she was an expert on human behavior. Otherwise, her life wouldn't be in shambles.

Nicole squeezed her back. "It's not your fault. I should be more firm in telling him to go away. But I don't have the heart to, not when I know he's also grieving."

Her sister might have lost her optimism, but she hadn't lost her heart. And if there was anything that gave Leah hope that things would work out all right for them, it was that all three of them remained steadfast in their belief in doing the right thing. So, what was the right thing when it came to the man who was interacting with her boys in a way they so desperately needed?

Leah entered the room, swallowing her pain as she firmly told herself that she could enjoy the gift of this moment.

"What are you guys doing?"

A wide grin filled Ryan's face. "We play horse."

Shane started to sit up, but Dylan grabbed his neck. "The phone didn't ring yet. It's still my turn."

Reaching around and patting Dylan on the leg, Shane said, "He has a point. I told the boys we could play horse, and I set a timer to let them know when their turn was over. You don't mind waiting until we finish, do you?"

She often used that tactic with them, giving them clear boundaries with which to set their expectations. It was nice to see that Shane automatically did the same. The only other person to do it was Nicole, and she had taught preschool for a living.

"Not at all. I've got to finish the garlic bread, and Erin isn't back yet. You guys finish your game, then you can join us in the kitchen."

She barely got the assent from Shane because the three of them had already jumped back into their game.

As she returned to the kitchen, Nicole linked arms with her. "I know we've all sworn off men, but it's nice to see a man who will play with the children for a change. Half of the moms in my classes complained that the dads weren't very active with their kids."

"Yes, but just because he'll entertain a couple of boys for a few minutes doesn't mean that's how he'll be as a father."

Nicole sighed. "True. It's amazing how people change when you get to know them. I'm sure when you and Jason first got together, you would have never imagined how things would end up."

No, she hadn't. Nicole had been the one to get a call from a concerned neighbor the first time Jason had been passed out, high on drugs, and the boys were screaming. Leah had been at work, and, as a salesperson in a busy store, hadn't been allowed personal calls. Sometimes Leah wondered if things would have turned out differently had the neighbor not been able to reach Nicole and called the police instead. Would

Jason have gotten help rather than fighting with Leah about it? Or would he have charmed them with lies and false promises the way he had everyone else?

It didn't matter. Jason was dead. And Leah was left to pick up all the pieces of all the broken things he'd left behind. Her sons would heal, and, even though it was nice to see them enjoying a man's company, their lives would not hinge upon him being there.

The two sisters finished preparing the meal. A few minutes later, Shane and the boys came in, laughing about horses.

Erin had texted to let them know she was going to be late and to go ahead and eat without her, so Leah started serving the meal, enjoying the camaraderie everyone seemed to share. Though earlier in the week it had annoyed her to be subject to Shane's easy grins and charming demeanor, it didn't bother her so much this evening. Maybe it was because he seemed just as focused on making her sons smile as he was on her.

After dinner, Nicole volunteered to clear the table so Leah and Shane could sit in the living room with the boys.

"Let's play horse again," Dylan said, tugging at Shane's hand.

"Not now," he said. "It's time for grown-up talk. Your mommy has some papers to go over with me, so we need to do our business, and if you're good, when we're done, we can find a game that everyone can play."

Dylan didn't argue, then he ran over to the train table where his brother was already playing.

"I would have killed to have a train set like that what I was a kid," Shane said.

Leah couldn't help smiling at the longing look he

gave the boys. "We started the collection as soon as I knew I was having a boy. It's expensive to buy the trains all at once, but if you buy them bit by bit and look for them at resale stores, you can often find pieces at reasonable prices. The train tables were all too expensive, so I built one based on plans I found online."

One thing she had learned in her marriage was that she was far more capable than she gave herself credit for.

"Your sister mentioned you were good with tools and things," he said, looking impressed. "How did that happen?"

"When my husband and I bought our first house, we both fell in love with an old Victorian that needed a lot of work. We didn't have much money, so we learned to do most of the work ourselves. Once you remodel a house, everything else is easy."

It was good to remember that her past with Jason wasn't all bad. She didn't want the bitterness to eat her up, and even though her sons were young, she wanted them to have happy stories about their father. Before his drug addiction had taken control of his life, he'd been a good person.

But that didn't mean she wasn't going to be guarded in her interactions with men in the future. Shane might be charming, and he might be good with her boys. But she wasn't going to let the charming smile he kept flashing at her distract her from what was truly important in her life.

Shane handed her a stack of papers. As she read through the contract, she already knew, without having to discuss it with her sisters, they would have to reject the offer. Most people would jump at the idea of taking money for nothing. But they weren't most people. They needed to make a living somehow, and even though Erin was excited about going to work again, it wasn't fair for Erin to have to support the whole household. Unfortunately, the amount Shane was giving them for the lease wouldn't be enough for them to survive on.

"What do you think?" Shane asked, an earnest look on his face. It seemed cruel to tell him no when he acted like he was doing them a favor.

"I'll have to talk to my sisters. It all sounds very reasonable though."

It did sound reasonable. The number was higher than what he'd paid Helen. But, sometimes, reasonable wasn't enough. Not when you needed so much.

Leah turned to watch the boys play with the trains. At least she hadn't had to sell those precious keepsakes. She'd done her best to keep the boys' belongings since they'd lost so much already. Their house, the playhouse and swing set she and Jason had built them, even their college fund. How Jason had managed to drain it for drugs without her finding out, she didn't know. She supposed it didn't matter. The money was gone.

"I can't believe you made that," Shane said. "While I know my way around a set of tools, I don't think I could come up with anything so detailed. It looks like you put a lot of effort into it."

"You'd be surprised at what a person can do when they put their mind to something. I know you're worried about us making it on our own. I'll admit we have much to learn. But each night, after we put the boys to bed, my sisters and I read the ranching books from Helen's library. We discuss what we learn and how it might apply to our ranch. That's how I learned to do so much work on my old house."

Looking around the room, Leah couldn't help but smile. "I've already done a number of much-needed repairs here. The back porch was falling down, and unsafe for the boys. Many of the windows were either sealed shut or leaked so badly that they wasted precious energy. I painted the room, refinished the floor, and I'm slowly working on updating the plumbing. And, of course, I've given the place a good scrubbing."

Shane nodded slowly. "Helen let things go over the past year. I did my best to help her, and a bunch of us from church put a new roof on the place a few months ago. But I know there was still a lot of work to be done."

He sounded so apologetic, like it was his responsibility to fix up the ranch. Odd, since Helen wasn't even his relative. Clearly, he took the idea of being a neighbor a little too seriously. Sure, it was nice to know that the old woman hadn't been alone and helpless in her later years. But Leah and her sisters were not helpless old women.

"We appreciate everything you've done, but now you know we can take care of ourselves. You probably think you're saving us, with your white horse and all, but we don't need saving."

She had to giggle at her own words because his horse literally was white. If she'd made up a stereotypical cowboy hero, he would look a lot like Shane.

Shane chuckled. "Actually, Squirt is a gray." Then

a more serious expression crossed his face. "And I'm doing nothing of the sort. I'm just being neighborly."

Neighborly. She'd admit that, in many ways, he had been helpful. But she didn't want to rely on him too much. At some point, he'd have his own life to live, his own children to take care of. She'd learned that the only person you could count on was yourself. And her sisters, of course, but that was because they'd spent so much of their lives with only each other to count on. So many people had come and gone, women the Colonel would gleefully announce as being their newest mother, most of whom never stuck around for very long. Not that Leah blamed them. As soon as she turned eighteen, she took the money she'd been saving from her after-school job and rented an apartment, taking her younger sisters with her so they would finally be out from under his thumb.

Why he let them, she didn't know. Probably because at the time his latest love was barely older than Leah. Though he'd always claimed he would send money to help with their support, most of the time those checks never materialized, and the sisters quickly learned how to take care of themselves. No one had ever saved them, at least not until Helen's surprise bequest. She'd given them enough to do what they had to, and they wouldn't be asking for more. Too many people had made too many promises to help, then failed to come through.

Leah knew what she had to do to take care of her family. It was what she had always done, and no matter how many charming offers came under the guise of being neighborly, she wasn't about to let her guard down.

Ryan came over and climbed into Shane's lap. He held out his favorite locomotive. "You pway wif me?"

His father certainly never had. He'd been too wrapped up in his own world to pay much attention to the little boy. Watching Shane take the train from her son was almost too much for Leah's heart to bear. She and her sisters had all agreed that they would be family enough for her children. And yet when Shane made a little choo-choo noise and Ryan giggled, it made Leah wonder if maybe she had been too hasty in saying she didn't need a man.

Dylan came over, holding another engine. "Are you done with your grown-up talk?"

Her heart melted at seeing the maturity in her son. They'd been working on boundaries, and to see her son respecting them made her think she was doing something right. Parenting was hard work, and though she knew her sisters didn't mind helping, sometimes she felt like a burden when the boys were being difficult. Getting Dylan under control meant she wouldn't have to take advantage of her sisters so much.

"We are. Do you want to show me what's happening in Happy Town?"

She took her son's hand and was pleased to see that Shane and Ryan followed. But just as quickly she had that thought, she wondered if she was making a mistake in letting this man she barely knew get too close to her boys.

As Dylan explained the setup, she stole a glance at Shane. He seemed like a solid, stable guy. But so had Jason. He'd even helped pay her sisters' college tuitions. Leah couldn't have predicted that the man she married would have broken his leg in a skiing accident, needing several surgeries and become addicted to pain pills, which later led to him becoming reliant on harder drugs.

"Mom! You're supposed to put the refrigerator car at the back of the line. We have a delivery to make to the other side of Happy Town."

She smiled at Dylan. "I'm so sorry. You're absolutely right. The people of Happy Town need their refrigerated goods."

"Happy Town?" Shane asked. "Why did you name it that?"

Dylan didn't look up from his enterprise. "Because sometimes bad things happen, and they're sad. But in Happy Town, it's okay to be happy because it's a safe place."

The way Shane looked at her made her feel funny inside. Leah looked away and saw Erin coming in the front door.

"Hello, everyone," Erin said, sounding cheerful as usual. "Sorry I'm late, but my interview went better than expected, and they wanted me to sort out a payroll issue so they can pay their men on time tomorrow. I can't believe what a big operation the Double R Ranch is. It makes our plans look puny. But what a great way to learn the business from the inside."

Shane stepped forward. "They don't run cattle the way they used to because Ricky has converted it to a holiday ranch to give city folks the cowboy experience. But you should still get some great ideas."

Why did he have to have an opinion on Erin's new job? It was like he had a personal stake in their success, which was ridiculous. The only people responsible for their family was them.

Unfortunately, Erin's cheerful expression didn't help Leah's cause. "Definitely. The guy must be at least eighty, but he can run circles around me. I'm excited to be working with him."

Okay, clearly Leah needed to dial back her defensiveness. Why couldn't she interact with Shane in the same easy way her sister did? And why did Shane keep looking at Leah? With every conversation they had, Shane always paid more attention to Leah than anyone else. It was unnerving, the way he seemed like he was always trying to figure her out. Why was he so interested in her?

Worse, why did the way he look at her send butterflies to her stomach? She absolutely could not—would not—let those stupid emotions influence her decisions ever again.

And yet, as Ryan ran back to Shane, holding trains in each hand, something deep inside her wished things could be different. She wished she were capable of trusting a man. And that she did have someone to share her life with. Though most of the time talking about things with her sisters was enough, she would be lying if she said she didn't miss curling up next to someone at night and being held as she talked about her dreams. But that fantasy had turned into a nightmare, and not even her deepest longing could make her willing to take that risk again.

Still, when Shane wrapped his arms around the little boy, part of Leah wished it was her.

She needed to spend as little time around Shane as possible. Clearly, there was something in his cologne messing with her head.

Chapter Four

Rejecting Shane's offer had been hard but necessary. But they needed more money. Which was why she sipped on a cup of black coffee while Erin and Nicole had lattes and muffins. The boys each had a cup of hot chocolate, a rare treat that she couldn't help letting her sisters get for them. But if she was going to have to live on her sister's charity, she'd make do on as little as possible.

In the corner of the café was an area with a sign that said Kiddie Corral, and it had small tables for the children as well as a selection of games and toys.

"You're crazy, not putting anything in your coffee." Erin looked around, then turned her attention back to Leah. "Speaking of crazy, how long are we supposed to wait for my potential accounting client? He's thirty minutes late."

Maybe Leah *was* crazy, thinking that making a fresh start would be easier than it was. It had all seemed so perfect, inheriting a ranch and moving to a new town to create a new life. Even without a house payment, she hadn't counted on things like having to pay eight hundred dollars to refill the propane tank.

"At least the trip to town isn't totally wasted," Leah said, looking over at the boys. A boy who appeared to be about Dylan's age had joined them, and they seemed to be playing nicely together.

Nicole reached forward and squeezed her hand. "It's nice to see them making friends. Hopefully, it's a sign of things to come."

A woman walked over to where the boys were and said something to them. Dylan pointed at Leah. She took a deep breath, stealing herself for the inevitable conversation. People usually didn't want to meet Dylan's mother unless he'd done something wrong.

"Hi," the woman said. "I'm Janie Roberts, Sam's mom. I hear you're new in town. Have you found a church yet? Sam is enjoying playing with Dylan, and we'd love for you to join us at Faith Community Church on Sunday."

Seriously? How many people in this town were going to invite her to church? From the way her sisters glared at her, she wasn't going to get away with saying no again. Her sisters were already mad that they didn't go last Sunday because Leah had needed them to help her with a plumbing issue that had popped up.

She owed it to them to at least give it a try.

"I'm Leah Holloway, and these are my sisters, Erin Drummond and Nicole Bell. We'd love to come to church. We've been meaning to, but there's so much work to be done on the ranch."

Janie smiled at her. "It's nice to meet you all. I know how it goes with having a lot to do. But it's like my dad always says, the work is easier when you take a little time to fill yourself with the Lord. He's the pastor of Faith Community Church."

Great. This woman was one of those perfect women whose lives were all about trying to get more followers for her father's flock.

"We'll be there Sunday," Leah said, gritting her teeth at the inevitable scene. They'd show up, people would start asking questions, and they would realize what sinners the whole family was and be done with them. It was best to just get it over with so they could get on with their lives.

Janie smiled. "I'm so glad to hear it. By the way our boys are playing, I'm sure your sons will really enjoy Sunday school."

Then Janie frowned, like she'd thought of a serious problem. "Oh. I know who you are. You're Helen's relatives, the ones who inherited her place. You must think we're terrible people, not welcoming you properly. My mom hasn't been well, and she asked me to bring a basket by, and to be honest, I keep forgetting. I know I'm not supposed to make excuses, but as a single mom, I'm struggling with managing everything and taking over some of my mom's duties."

"You're a single mom?" The question slipped out of Leah's mouth before she could take it back. Erin kicked her under the table.

"I'm sorry, that was rude. I don't know where that came from."

Janie shrugged. "It's okay. People make a lot of assumptions about me being the pastor's daughter, but I've made my share of mistakes. We all do. Which is why anyone should feel comfortable coming to our church."

Could she feel any worse? The poor woman probably had to defend herself a lot because of her father's job, and here she was, doing it to some stranger.

"You're right," Leah said. "I hate it when all people see when they look at me is a poor widow. I'm sorry for labeling you."

Janie pulled up a chair to their table and sat. "Like I said, it's okay. I've heard worse, and I'd rather people be honest with me then pretend everything is all right while they're secretly judging me. It sounds like we have a lot in common, trying to raise children on our own and rise above the talk. I'm sure it's scary, going to a new church and worrying about people judging you. But I hope it'll be easier knowing you have a friend."

"That means a lot," Erin said. "We're all a little gun-shy, but I remember coming here as a child and how much I loved the church. I'm hoping my sisters and I will feel the same again."

Leah looked over at her sister and saw the longing on her face. She'd seen it last time they were here in the café and had quickly forgotten. She owed it to Erin to give her something to heal the pain she carried.

"I'm willing to give it a try," Nicole said. "Who knows, maybe we'll find someone who can help us learn ranching. Don't get me wrong. I know Shane has said he'd help us, but he's got every reason in the world for us to fail. He needs our land for his cattle."

Janie gave them a startled look. "Shane would never do that. I've known him all my life, and if he says he's going to help you, he's going to help you. I know you guys are from the city, but here we look out for each other."

The idea was definitely foreign to them. But Leah didn't know this woman well enough to tell her just how badly everyone in their lives had always let them down.

"That sounds good," Erin said. "You're right. Things were different where we came from, and it's hard for us to trust someone new. We'll reserve judgment on Shane until we have all the facts."

"And some cows," Nicole muttered. "I still can't believe you guys came home last week empty-handed."

"Why would you buy cows now?" Janie asked. "Not many people are selling in the beginning of summer. If they are, you've got to suspect there's something wrong with the herd."

Exactly what Shane had said. And maybe, had they inherited the ranch in the spring or in the fall, they might have had better options. But if they waited until the fall to get their cows, they might not have the money.

"How else are we supposed to have a cattle ranch?" Nicole asked, sounding annoyed.

Janie let out a sigh. "If I were you, I'd wait until fall. Lease your pasture to Shane for the summer, buy what cows the other ranchers can't afford to feed over the winter, hopefully some pregnant ones, then in the spring sell the babies, keeping a few for yourself."

She made it sound so easy, like it didn't matter if they waited an extra few months for much-needed income. But they didn't have the luxury of time. They'd barely make it on the timeline they'd planned.

"Thanks for your advice," Erin said. "We'll keep it in mind."

It was frustrating that everyone seemed so intent

on discouraging her and her sisters and dispensing unwanted advice.

Fortunately, Janie didn't seem like she had any intention of pressing the issue. "I hate to run out on you, but I've got to be somewhere. You'll sit with me at church on Sunday, right?"

With the way her sisters' eyes were on her, Leah didn't dare say no. "Of course. It'll be nice to see a familiar face."

Once Janie left, they cleared their table so they could leave, as well. No sense in waiting for Erin's no-show client. They started toward the door, but an older man got out of his chair and stopped them.

"I couldn't help overhearing your conversation with Janie," he said. "While it's true people normally aren't selling cattle in the middle of summer, sometimes a rancher has to do what's necessary. And, not to speak bad about a neighbor, but everyone knows that Shane is the world's biggest tightwad. I'm sure he's low-balling you on your land lease. Helen gave it to him dirt cheap because he was like a son to her. Everyone knows your place has the most water and best grass."

She'd wanted to believe that Shane was being a good guy and that he was looking out for them. Was it weird to feel sick at knowing she might have been right about him? It was so frustrating, hearing different descriptions about the man, and not knowing what to believe, especially with her trust issues.

"We appreciate your candor," Erin said. "What do we do about the cattle? Is there someone willing to lease our land for a higher price so we can wait until fall to buy our cows?"

The man smiled. "I've got some for sale. My mother

is in New Jersey, and her health is failing. It's hard for me to keep going back and forth, so I want to sell my herd. But everyone I know has all the cows they need, and they can't afford any more. If you ladies take them off my hands, it would solve both our problems. I'd even be willing to sell them for less than market price. With what I'm paying in airfare, selling the cows, even at a discount, would save me a lot of money."

His story tugged at Leah's heart. What would it be like, going back and forth across the country to take care of a sick relative while trying to maintain a ranch? And getting cows at a discount made his offer really tempting.

"That sounds great," she said. "But we don't even know your name."

"Harold Stein. You might have seen my ranch off the highway leading into town."

They drove past that ranch every time they went to town. The boys liked to count the cows they saw in the pasture. Wouldn't it be funny to have those same cows?

"It does sound great," Erin said. "However, my sisters and I need to do some talking. Why don't you put an offer together and we'll consider it?"

Harold smiled. "I certainly will. I'll run something by your place in the morning."

"Thank you so much. Regardless of what we decide, I hope you understand how much we appreciate your offer." Leah smiled at him and held her hands out for the boys. "We'd best get going."

As they exited the coffee shop, Nicole leaned into her. "This sounds amazing. We should have taken the offer on the spot. What if someone else decides they want the cows?"

"Then they weren't the cows for us. We don't even know how much he wants for them." Leah didn't want to crush her hopes, but they didn't have all the facts. Even at below market price, could they afford what he wanted?

"I'm sure you're right." Nicole let out a long sigh. "But it just seems so cruel to be this close to our dream and not get it. I know I want the ranch to be a working one more than the two of you because of my love for animals, but I'm starting to get frustrated that we don't have anything yet."

She shared her sister's frustration, but she lacked her sister's blind trust in people. If only there were a clear solution to their problems.

Everyone kept wanting her to go to church and believe in God and all that nonsense. Well, if there was a God, then maybe He should make a way for the cow situation to work out. A herd of cheap cows would go a long way toward making their ranch successful and proving to Leah there really was a God who cared about them.

Shane looked at the sad-eyed bay mare standing before him. He'd talked Bobby down to fifteen hundred for the retired barrel-racing horse, but he was still sure Bobby had gotten the better end of the deal. This old horse didn't look like she'd done much of anything for years, but he supposed that's what made her perfect for the two little boys getting out of their mother's beat-up car.

Maybe he was too soft, but as the boys ran toward him, he couldn't call this purchase a mistake.

He stepped away from the rail he had the horse tied on and walked toward the boys. "Remember what I said about running and making too much noise around the horses."

The boys immediately stopped.

"Sorry, Mister Shane." Dylan hung his head.

"Sowwy," Ryan said.

"It's okay. But we need to remember the rules in the future."

As the boys nodded eagerly, he looked over at their mother. Leah hung back, looking a little more cheerful than he'd seen in the past.

"Leah? Would you like to join us?"

The smile she gave him was warm, bringing an odd sensation to his chest. Almost like she was hugging him from afar. What had changed so dramatically in their lives over the past few days? He'd caught a glimpse of them in church on Sunday, but hadn't had the chance to speak with them. He supposed it didn't matter, but he found himself wanting to know more. It seemed like the weight that had been upon her in their previous meetings was gone.

"Yes. I was just trying to give you space so the boys knew that when it comes to horses, you're in charge."

He wasn't expecting her to give him so much authority, not when she'd made it clear that she didn't like him interfering with her parenting. But he wasn't going to argue. Not when she was right. He'd been afraid that having the boys come over to see his horses would turn into a power struggle. Maybe he'd judged her too harshly. After all, they'd had a good time the other evening, playing with the trains.

"I appreciate that," he said. Then he turned to the boys. "Rule number one, you can't go near the horses without an adult present."

The boys murmured their agreement, and as he continued explaining the rules, he noticed the respectful way the boys looked at him. Like they were listening. It was hard to believe these were the same boys who'd acted up the first time he met them. Aside from that one day, he'd found the boys well-behaved and delightful. Maybe he'd been too hasty in judging them, too.

Once he explained the rules to the boys, he held his hand out to them. "Would you like to pet my horse?"

"What's his name?" Dylan asked.

Shane smiled. "Her name is Belle."

"A girl?" Dylan looked disgusted. "Cowboys don't ride girl horses. They ride stallions."

He chuckled at the little boy's indignation. Somewhere in the boy's education, he'd learned that stallions were boy horses. But he obviously hadn't learned everything.

"Dylan! Remember what we talked about. There is nothing wrong with girls. We need to be respectful when we talk about girls." Leah gave Shane an apologetic look. "Sorry about that. He's just now learning that there is a difference between boys and girls, and for some reason he seems to have something against girls."

Even though Leah seemed seriously disturbed by the idea, Shane fought the urge to laugh. It must be horrifying for three women raising boys to have to deal with some of the quirks they didn't understand.

Shane bent down in front of the boys. "Girls are just as important as boys. Your mom is a girl. What would you do without her?"

"She's not a girl. She's a mom." Dylan gave him another disgusted look. "For a grown-up, you don't know anything."

"Manners," Leah said.

Dylan turned to her. "But he called you a girl. Girls are stinky."

"Who told you that?" she asked.

"I learned it in Sunday school. My friend Joshua said that all girls are stinky. And if I want to play with him, I have to say girls are stinky, too."

The exasperation on Leah's face told Shane that she was at a loss for how to handle the situation. Having done his own rotation teaching the Sunday-school class, he knew the boy Dylan was talking about. His dad was one of those loudmouthed jerks that made decent men look bad.

"That might be what Joshua thinks about girls," Shane said, "but if you want to be a cowboy, then you need to know that cowboys always treat girls right. We treat all people and animals with respect, because that is the cowboy way."

Not all cowboys followed that philosophy, much to Shane's dismay. But he liked to think of himself as one of the good guys, and, hopefully, he could be a role model to these boys, and hit home that men like Joshua and his father were not examples to live by.

"Will you teach me more about being a cowboy?" Dylan asked.

"Of course I will." He looked over to see that Ryan had plopped himself down in the dirt to play in it. He was too young for philosophical discussions about what it meant to be a good man, but, God willing, his brother would learn and pass it on to him.

"Do I get a cowboy hat?"

Shane stole a glance at Leah, who had gone over to Ryan and handed him a toy car out of her purse.

"That's for when you graduate cowboy lessons," he said, smiling at Dylan. "Do you want cowboy lessons?"

Dylan nodded enthusiastically, his hair flopping wildly.

"The first lesson is what I just told you. We treat all people and animals with respect. So you should apologize to your mother for calling girls stinky."

"And then I get my hat?"

He had to give the boy credit for being persistent. "There are still a lot of cowboy lessons to be learned. But this is a good start."

"How many lessons are there?"

He hadn't expected the question, nor was he prepared to give an answer. Leah wouldn't appreciate him buying her son a cowboy hat without her permission.

"A lot," he finally said. "But I need to talk to your mother about cowboy lessons before I go making any deals."

Before Dylan could press him further, Leah returned to his side, holding Ryan. "Someone needs to be changed. Do you mind if I go inside and take care of it?"

"He's such a baby," Dylan said. "Why can't he use the potty like a big boy?"

Shane shook his head at Dylan. "Remember what I

said about respecting people? You don't call someone a baby if you're respecting them."

For a moment, he thought Dylan was going to throw a tantrum. But then he nodded and turned to his mother. "I'm sorry for calling girls stinky." Then he looked at his brother. "I'm sorry for calling you a baby."

Leah gave him a surprised look, and he was once again warmed by her smile. She turned her attention to Dylan. "I accept your apology."

"Let's go inside," Shane said. "You can take care of what you need, and maybe this cowpoke here can help me with some lemonade."

Dylan puffed out his chest. "And then I can be a cowboy and have my own cowboy hat?"

The kid was harder to shake than one of those little yappy dogs.

"I told you, I have to talk to your mother about cowboy lessons. But the more you ask, the longer it's going to take."

Though his face fell into a pout, the little boy followed them into the house. Shane showed Leah to the bathroom, then he led Dylan into the kitchen.

"Let's get some lemonade for everyone. I've also got some cookies."

"Cookies? Mom never lets us have cookies."

At the excited look on Dylan's face, Shane realized he probably shouldn't have said anything. He should've waited to privately ask Leah if it was all right to offer the boys a cookie. It had been too long since he'd spent time with Gina and Natalie for him to remember all the nuances of parenting. That, and Leah's parenting was different from Gina's. Gina had stepped back and let him take over, but Leah was always clearly the one in charge.

He'd already made the lemonade in anticipation of the visit, but including Dylan in another way would give the boy something to do. Shane pulled a chair up to the counter, then opened the cupboard where he kept his glasses.

"Why don't you pick which glass everyone gets to have?"

He didn't have anything fancy, just mismatched glasses he'd collected over the years, mostly from garage sales and flea markets. Gina used to get on him about it, saying he needed to be more of a grown-up and have proper dishes. But it wasn't like he was entertaining the president or anything like that. He just needed the basics.

Dylan reached for one of the mugs. "I want that one."

It had to be that mug. The one Natalie had given him for Christmas right before Gina had taken her and left. World's Greatest Dad. According to Gina, Shane had been the closest thing to a dad that Natalie had ever had. Not that it mattered when Gina decided to leave, because she refused to let Shane remain in contact with Natalie. He often prayed that whatever guy Gina ended up with would be as good to Natalie as Shane had been. Or even better.

"That's my special mug," Shane said. "It's for drinking coffee, not lemonade."

"But I like it. It has a horse on it. And a handle. Handles make it easier to drink."

Dylan was starting to whine. He usually didn't give in to kids like this, but he felt selfish for refusing a kid something as simple as a mug. It wasn't like it was made of gold.

"Do you promise to be careful?"

Dylan nodded.

"All right then. Now let's pick out the glasses for your mom and brother."

Dylan chose a variety of glasses for everyone else, making Shane feel even sillier for making a big deal out of a mug. The little boy had picked one with purple flowers for his mother because it was her favorite color. He'd chosen a blue plastic glass for his brother, saying that Ryan still broke things. And then he'd magnanimously told Shane to choose his favorite.

By the time Leah returned to the kitchen, carrying a plastic bag, they had the lemonade poured and set out on the table with the cookies.

"Do you have an outdoor trashcan I can put this in?" she asked, looking around.

"I'll take it," he said. "You and Ryan have a seat. Dylan helped me get everything set up."

She looked at her son with such pride that Shane was glad he'd let Dylan have the special mug. "I'm glad to see you're being so helpful."

The little squeeze she gave her son warmed his heart. Leah was a good mom, and her boys would grow into good men because of it.

"Mister Shane is teaching me how to be a cowboy. That way, when we pick up our cows from that man, I can help you take care of them."

Shane stopped at the door. "What cows from what man?"

"We still haven't decided for sure," Leah said, giving her son a look before turning her attention to

Shane. He might not know much about the family, but he knew when a mother was telling her son he'd said too much.

"We met a man in town, Harold Stein. He's got to sell his cattle, so he can be with his ailing mother in New Jersey. He offered them to us at below market price. It's a little more than we were budgeting for, but it's a much larger herd than we'd planned on. We're still trying to see if we can make it work."

The situation reeked, and it wasn't because of the dirty diaper he still held in his hand. He knew all about Harold Stein's herd. All the ranchers around here did. And not a one of them would touch those cows with a thousand-foot pole.

"I hate to burst your bubble," he said slowly. "But you don't want those cows. There's already one confirmed case of Bangs disease in that herd, and the rest are under quarantine until the vet can clear them. If you buy those cows, you can't bring them or their babies to market for at least a year. And that's if they continue to test negative."

Leah paled, and Shane hated that he'd had to deliver such bad news. But at least she knew now, before she'd sunk the precious little money she had into a herd that would probably cost her more in the long run.

Unfortunately, she didn't look all that thankful.

In fact, as he stepped out to the trash, giving her a minute to collect her thoughts, he just hoped that he being the one to tell her wouldn't cause her to put a wall up again.

Chapter Five

Leah fought the urge to pull out her phone and look up Bangs disease. It sounded like a bad hairstyle, not something for cows. She hated it when others did that, and she tried to be fully present when she was with someone else. But Shane had just dropped a bomb with more megatons than she had the capacity to process on her own.

"I'm sorry," Shane said again, pouring her a cup of coffee. The lemonade had been fine for a social call, but he'd brewed a pot upon returning to the house.

It seemed so unfair that they'd been given a chance to get their ranch up and running, only to have it taken from them again.

"I don't even understand what this disease is," Leah said, trying to remember if she'd read anything about it in her ranching books.

"It's a highly contagious and deadly disease for cattle."

As he explained the disease and how it affected cattle, Leah felt numb. Shane was right; it would ruin them if these cattle had it.

"But you don't know for sure if the cows have it, right?" She looked up at him, hoping there was some way out of this mess. A way for her ranch to work.

He picked up one of the crayons Dylan had dropped and sat across from her, handing her son the crayon. Dylan seemed to have really taken to Shane and was busily drawing him a picture. It was nice to see her son so excited about interacting with others like this.

"Maybe," Shane said slowly. "What we do know is that Harold sold one of the other ranchers a cow a few months ago, and it tested positive. A few more in Harold's herd were then examined and had to be culled because they also had it. The rest are testing negative right now, but sometimes it can take up to a year for a positive result. Once you get that positive, the cow has to be put down to prevent it from spreading. Any other animal it's come into contact with has to be in quarantine for a year, just to be safe."

A few months ago. Did that mean there was hope?

"How common is it for a positive test result after a year?"

He let out a long sigh, and she figured she wouldn't like his answer. But he didn't understand how much having a successful ranch meant to her. To her family.

"The longer you go without testing positive, the less likely the cows are to get it. But it's still possible to have the disease show up a year later, which is why every precaution has to be taken. An outbreak can destroy a ranch, and the Department of Agriculture has strict rules in place to keep it from spreading. I know you want to believe that things will turn out all right, and maybe they will. But it's not worth the risk when everything you have is riding on having a healthy herd."

So it wasn't necessarily going to ruin them. If the herd continued testing negative, then everything would be fine. But they'd still have to wait until their year was up before being able to sell them. Which meant that they wouldn't see a profit for a long time.

Even if the cows didn't have this disease… Leah shook her head. Why did it seem like everything was stacked against them?

Shane reached across the table and took her hand. "I know it's a real blow to think you have a lead on a great herd, then to find it's not going to work. But my offer still stands. I'd be happy to lease your land, give you some extra income while you learn more about ranching, and then when they have the big sales in the fall, I'll help you pick out some cows. Be patient. It'll work out."

Easy enough for him to say. He wasn't struggling to make ends meet, to pull his own weight.

"Hey! I was using the red!" Dylan smacked his brother.

Ryan started to wail.

It was past Ryan's naptime, and the boys had had an exciting day. Dylan usually took a rest when his brother napped, and it did wonders for the boys. She should have known better than to mess with their schedule, and the meltdown was proof of it.

"Boys," she said, using her firmest tone. "That's enough. Dylan, we don't hit. Apologize to your brother."

Dylan started to cry. "But he stole my crayon."

"Remember what I said about cowboys being kind to others," Shane said gently.

Who was he to step in and try to discipline her sons? She didn't need his interference.

Ryan's sobs grew louder, which made Dylan's wailing worse. Definitely a mistake to delay naptime.

"Boys."

They both looked up at her warning. Ryan yawned. "Mama."

She held her arms out to him, and he crawled into them. He immediately put his head on her shoulder. He'd be asleep within minutes.

"I'm waiting for your apology, Dylan." She looked at her older son, who still looked defiant, tears rolling down his cheeks.

"He stole my crayon."

"We don't hit." She spoke firmly. It was probably a lost cause, but she had to keep enforcing this rule. Dylan liked to lash out with violence when things didn't go his way, something he'd learned from his father, and she had to break him of the habit.

"Stealing is wrong, too," Dylan said, picking up his mug and throwing it across the room.

As the mug shattered on the tile floor, Leah felt sick. She should have paid better attention to the time and taken the boys home before the meltdown occurred.

"I'm so sorry about the mug," she said, turning to Shane. "I'll replace it."

She was expecting the usual response when her kids broke something. Like, "Control your kids," or "It's just a mug," but the expression on Shane's face… It was like Dylan had destroyed his most precious family heirloom. But that was ridiculous. People didn't let children play with family heirlooms. And it was a silly mug. With World's Greatest Dad written on it. Shane didn't have any kids, so it couldn't have any special meaning to him.

Except he looked utterly devastated.

"Really. I'm so sorry," she said again. But from the way he looked, she didn't think a simple apology was going to cut it.

She shifted Ryan to her side, and sure enough, he was almost asleep. "Dylan, we should go. If this is how you're going to act when you visit our friend, then you're not going to come here anymore."

Her words seemed to jolt Shane out of whatever funk having his cup broken had put him in. "It's not necessary for you to go. I just need to get a broom."

Leah sighed. "I'm sorry. I should have offered to help you clean up. Ryan's almost asleep, and I think it would be best if I got the boys home to rest."

Now he really must think her a terrible mom. But it couldn't be helped. She was doing the best she could. It just didn't seem to be good enough.

Shane forced down the frustration and pain at seeing the shattered pieces of the mug on his kitchen floor. Helen would have told him it was just a thing, a worthless object. And in some ways she would have been correct. But that mug represented so much to him. It had been the only thing Natalie had given him that he'd been able to keep. Most of the pictures had been taken when Gina left. The few that remained had been destroyed when his water heater had burst. An unfortunate accident, just as this was. But seeing his mug destroyed hurt more.

"I'm sorry, Mister Shane," Dylan said, tears running down his face.

Leah looked over at him. "I'd be happy to replace it," she said. "I'm truly sorry. The boys are off their schedule, and while it doesn't excuse their behavior, I hope it helps you understand."

She turned to her son and held out her hand. "We should get going."

"I want to ride the horse." Dylan's wails grew louder.

The little boy in Leah's arms shifted but did not wake. At least someone was finding peace in this moment.

"Not today." Her voice held the same firm-but-patient tone he'd noticed when he'd first met them. "Maybe some other time."

She reached to take her son's hand, but he turned and kicked her. From the way she recoiled, he could tell it was hard.

"That's not okay," she said, her voice wavering. She sounded like she was trying to hold back tears, and she was doing a good job of it.

Leah turned to Shane. "Could you keep your eye on him for a moment please? I'd like to get Ryan in his car seat, then I'll be back for Dylan."

He nodded, recognizing the despondent look on her face. He'd seen it often enough on Gina, who found parenting overwhelming at best. At least Leah had her sisters to help her. But still, as he watched her leave, he couldn't help wondering why he always found himself with women who needed him too much to love him.

"Well, go on," Dylan said, giving him such a harsh glare it was hard to believe a child was looking at him.

Shane didn't say anything but instead turned to grab the broom so he could sweep up the mess.

"I said come on. I know you're going to hit me, just like *he* did."

The boy's words made him feel sick. What happened behind closed doors with their family? And who was "he?" Dylan's father? Leah said he was dead.

Before he could give it much more thought, the small boy charged him, screaming, "Hit me."

Shane didn't have time to react, other than to wrap his arms around the small boy and let him kick at him and punch him while he screamed, "I'm bad! Hit me."

But he didn't. It might have started with a stolen crayon, then a broken mug, but this little boy's anger was about so much more. As he held the still-kicking-and-screaming child, he looked out the window to see Leah still buckling her son into the car. Is this what she would do?

He remembered their first meeting and how she had sat quietly through that fit. Shane didn't have that option, so hopefully this was the right decision.

"We don't hit the people we love," he said softly. "I'm not going to hit you."

But Dylan continued screaming and hitting him. For a moment, Dylan's hold loosened, but then he turned and bit Shane. With a surprised yelp, Shane pulled away from the little boy. He looked at Dylan and could see the fear in his eyes. His heart broke when he thought of what must have happened to put it there.

The door opened, and Leah entered. Dylan ran to

her. "He hit me," Dylan said. "He grabbed me, and he hurt me."

Leah looked at her son, then over at Shane, who was still holding his arm from being bitten.

"I didn't hit him," Shane said. "I would never hurt a child."

She didn't even glance at him but turned to Dylan. "Where did he hit you?"

Was she serious? She was taking the kid's word for it?

Dylan began to sob again. "Everywhere."

"Everywhere?" she asked.

Dylan nodded.

"Are you hurt?"

Dylan sniffled and nodded.

"Do I get to say anything?" Shane asked, looking at Leah.

She shook her head. "I'm not doing this right now. He needs to get home and have some quiet time. I should have known better than to come here."

He couldn't read the expression on her face, except that it looked like she might have been spending a little too much time sucking on lemons.

Turning to look at him, she said, "Don't worry. I'm not going to say anything to anyone. You won't be getting a call from the police or child protective services."

What was she talking about? Why would she say something like that? Did she really think he would hurt her child? Was it her way of warning him that the next time Dylan made such an accusation, she would?

Before he could give voice to any of these questions, Leah was gone. He watched her help her son into the car, then she got into the driver's seat and drove away. Surely, this wasn't how it was going to be.

He finished picking up the pieces of the mug, which was too shattered to be repaired. Kind of like the pieces of his heart after Gina had left. A good reminder that whatever this mess with Leah was, he'd be better off not getting involved. And yet, there had been moments when he'd thought…

No, he wasn't going to think about those things. Just because she was the first woman to catch his eye in a long time didn't mean she'd be the last. Her circumstances were a complication he didn't need in his life. He'd been doing well enough on his own the past few years.

It wasn't his job to interfere, fix or even rescue Leah. He'd see her in church on Sundays, and that would have to be enough for him. He had to trust that God would do whatever work with Leah that needed to be done.

But even as he tried to justify washing his hands of her, the image of Helen, frail and weak, came to mind as she told him how desperately her girls needed to be loved and that she was counting on him to be there for them, and he felt like his excuses were nothing more than a cop-out.

But Leah wasn't the only sister. Surely, he could reach out to the other two and be their friend. That would be a safer option. Even though he'd enjoyed his conversations with Erin and Nicole, he didn't feel the same level of connection to them the way he did Leah. It was like he was a glutton for punishment.

And as he went outside to throw away the broken bits of ceramic, he saw the horse in the pen that reminded him what a sap he was. He'd never been one for easy. At least in that he was consistent.

So how did he keep his promise to Helen without getting his heart broken?

Chapter Six

Leah exited the feed store, her heart heavy. Nicole had been offered a job at the local day care center, giving them another source of income. She should be relieved but instead it left her with an additional sense of guilt. With both of her sisters gainfully employed and the boys at home, how could Leah contribute to the family finances?

She'd stopped by the feed store, hoping they'd be hiring. If she worked there, she could talk to some of the ranchers and get their advice. But because she was only available to work two days a week, based on her sisters' schedules, they weren't interested in hiring her. They needed someone who could be more reliable, able to work more hours.

The story of her life.

She'd had the same issue with every other job she'd tried to get over the past few years. A lot of people wanted to call her lazy, unwilling to work. It wasn't that at all. With two boys to care for, even with her sisters' help, she simply didn't have the same options for availability others did. Even if she put her boys in the day care her sister worked at, she wouldn't make enough money to pay that bill. How could you spend fifteen dollars an hour on day care if you only made ten?

As she walked toward her car, she spotted Harold. He jogged over to her.

"I hadn't heard back from you about my cattle. Are you still interested in buying them?"

She'd hoped that by not calling him back he would understand she wasn't interested.

"Sorry, I've been busy. But I did some research, and I heard that your cows have Bangs. I don't think we can afford to take on such a challenge."

Those few words made her stomach hurt. She'd told the truth, and from the look on Harold's face he didn't disagree with her words.

"One of my cows that I sold earlier in the year tested positive. That doesn't mean my whole herd has it. Yes, the herd is in quarantine, but it will be lifted soon, and I have every confidence that my cows will be fine. Over the past few months, we've had no other positive cases. The Department of Agriculture is exercising an abundance of caution, but everything will be fine."

He sounded so confident. She had done some reading on the disease, and while it was true that the longer they went without a positive test result, the more likely it was to continue being negative, there was always the chance things could go wrong. It was a huge risk, especially given that if she was wrong, it would ruin them.

"I'm sure it will," she said. "But given my lack of experience with cattle and our tight finances, it's not wise for me to make such a purchase right now. I appreciate the offer, and I'm sure it's more than generous. But Shane said—"

"Shane again? I should have known he was behind your refusal. He's mad because I sold the bull he wanted to someone else. It wasn't my fault that he couldn't come up with the money in time. He's held a grudge against me ever since."

Shane didn't seem like the kind of person to hold a grudge, especially over something so trivial. But how well did she know Shane?

She gave Harold an apologetic smile. "Even so, I'm afraid it's more than our budget will allow. I know you're giving us a good deal, and if we had more money, I'd consider it more seriously. But we simply can't afford so much right now."

Harold looked thoughtful, then he nodded. "I understand. I remember when I was getting started, and what the lean years looked like."

He hesitated, then looked around. "Truth be told, my finances are tight, as well. Having to deal with the added expenses of helping my mother, her medical bills and constantly traveling back to see her has been difficult. I don't know how long I can keep feeding my cattle. My land isn't as good as yours for grazing, so I have to supplement."

She could understand the dilemma.

"I'll tell you what," he said. "I'll cut my price in half. Don't tell anyone I offered it to you, because they'll say I'm an old fool. But you could use a little help, and I'm desperate. You'll never get a better deal anywhere."

She'd done enough research to know that the price he'd already offered her was a really good deal. But to cut it in half? She'd be stupid to say no. Yes, there was the potential that some of the cows might have a disease, a deadly disease that could wipe out the entire herd, but it had been long enough since the last diagnosis that chances were it was a healthy herd. Just as he said.

Harold gave her a gentle smile. "Ask anyone else in town. They'll all tell you that I would never cheat anyone. Shane is the only one with anything against me."

When she'd talked to her sisters about not accepting Harold's original deal, they'd told her that they trusted her judgment, though Nicole was a bit cranky over the idea.

Once again, she sent a quick prayer to the God she wasn't sure cared about her, and hoped that somehow He would see fit to answer her prayers that she wasn't making a mistake.

"All right. You've got a deal." She kept her voice firm, hoping she didn't sound as doubtful as she felt.

Harold smiled. "You won't regret it. I know that this is going to be the start of a wonderful life for you and your family."

He stuck out his hand, but then his cell phone rang, and he looked down at it. "Excuse me."

As he answered the call, he stepped away. From the expression on his face, she could tell that it wasn't good news. She waited for him to finish the call, and then he returned to her. "My mother has taken a turn for the worse. I'm going to drive to Denver and get on the next flight. As soon as I'm able, I'll be in touch with paperwork and transfer information."

Before Leah could answer, he turned and walked down the street to a truck. Whatever was wrong with his mother, she hoped she'd be all right. She sent another prayer for the woman, hoping she hadn't already asked God for too much. She didn't know what to pray for, but she hoped that He would know what to do.

Before she could head back to her car, Shane approached. "Hi, Leah. I saw you talking to Harold. I take it you told him you weren't going to be buying his cattle."

Just the person she didn't want to see. Not only was she going to have to tell him she agreed to buy the cows, but she was dreading having to discuss what had happened at his house. She'd thought that Dylan was beyond his tantrums and games. Because of an incident at a previous school, he learned that if he claimed an adult hurt him, the attention for his wrongdoing was gone, and the adult got in trouble. At least temporarily.

She'd hoped that by reassuring Shane that she wasn't going to call the authorities on him, he would understand and everything would be all right.

Instead, he kept calling and leaving messages for her. And she didn't want to talk to him. Not about that. Especially if it meant confessing how bad their lives had been leading up to Jason's death and during the aftermath. People didn't understand the shame, and everyone wanted to blame her for not doing enough, not being enough, and for allowing it to happen.

For now, she'd choose the easier of the two conversations.

"Actually, I've accepted his offer," she said.

Still a difficult conversation, but at least this one wasn't as painful and personal as the other one.

"You did what?" He shook his head. "I don't think

you understand what you're getting into. The cost of testing, putting down sick cattle, feeding cattle you may have to eventually put down and not being able to sell them. I know you're eager to get started, but you have no idea what a mistake you're making."

Arguments she already had made with herself. "He said it was only one cow. It was months ago. The likelihood of it being his whole herd is slim. And he offered me a better price. This is the best opportunity I have for starting my ranch, and I'm going to take it."

Maybe Shane didn't understand what it was like to be so desperate. At least if they got the cattle, she could take care of them, and then, when they were allowed to sell them, they would have an income to show for it. She could contribute to the family in a meaningful way. No one in this small town was hiring, and those who were weren't interested in someone who couldn't give them much time.

"It will be worth the risk," she said. "I've been reading up on cow diseases, and we can handle it. Besides, the price for the cows is ridiculously low, well beneath market price."

"And so it should be," Shane said. "Anyone buying those cows is taking a huge risk. I know you aren't from around here, and you have no ranching experience. But please, Leah, reconsider. Don't buy those cows."

Tears stung the backs of her eyes. He didn't get it. He didn't understand the importance of the situation.

"I have to do something. My sisters both have jobs. But what is there for me, with children to raise? I have to bring in income for the family. I know it's not instant money, but at least it will be something in the future."

The gentle look he gave her was almost too much to bear. "I can understand that. But this isn't a guaranteed long-term plan. Ranching at its best is a risk, but this is insanity."

He acted like she was a child who didn't know her own mind. But if this endeavor was successful, the profit margin wouldn't just keep the family afloat, but would give her the much-needed funds for Dylan to go back to therapy. He'd been making progress with his last therapist, but with finances what they were, she couldn't keep paying for it. And after what had happened at Shane's house, her son obviously needed more.

"I know you're trying to help," she said, letting out an audible sigh. "I don't think you understand how desperate I am."

He shook his head slowly. "I understand more than you think. But what will you do when your plan fails?"

She refused to consider that option. She would find a way to make this work. She had to.

"Maybe, if you weren't so discouraging about my plans, I could find a way."

He stared at her for a moment, looking her up and down. "Are you serious about wanting to be a rancher?"

"Isn't that what I've been trying to tell you?"

"You'd be amazed at how many people move out here, thinking it would be fun to have a ranch, and then realize they're not up for the work. I'd like to propose another solution. Wait to get the cows. Come work for me. I'll teach you what you need to know.

At least give it the summer. In the fall, you can buy a herd of your own."

It sounded good. Maybe she had been too hasty in judging him. If he helped her, she could learn what she needed to do with her herd. Even if these other cows turned out to be diseased, the loss wouldn't be as devastating with income from a job to fall back on.

"What would the hours be? My biggest problem is finding childcare for the boys. None of the jobs around here pay enough for me to be able to afford day care, and both my sisters are working now."

Shane looked thoughtful for a moment. "Most ranchers work with their children running around. It's how I learned. But…"

He hesitated, and she knew what was coming next.

"We need to get the behavior under control. What happened the other day at my house—"

"I told you, I'm not calling the authorities. There's no need."

Shane made a noise. "That's the problem. You say you're not going to tell the authorities. About what? You didn't even hear me out. I can't stand accused of wrongdoing when I don't even get to defend myself."

It hadn't occurred to her that he would think that she thought him guilty. She'd been so busy trying to defuse the situation with Dylan that she hadn't considered how Shane was interpreting her words.

"I'm sorry. It was my way of telling you that I wasn't agreeing with Dylan's accusations, without riling him up further. Things got bad…" She hesitated. How much was safe to share with him?

Leah took a deep breath. "Things were bad with my late husband, and I didn't realize how it had affected

Dylan until it was too late. He's got some behavior issues that we're working on, but it's not always easy in an unfamiliar place."

Though Shane gave her an encouraging smile, there wasn't anything for her to smile about, not standing in the middle of the street along the tiny line of buildings that made up downtown Columbine Springs.

"I'm trying not to judge you. But you make it hard when you close yourself off. If we're working together and you're bringing the boys, you've got to level with me."

Level with me. An easy enough request, but she'd been burned before.

Shane gestured at the café. "Why don't I buy you a cup of coffee and we can talk about it? Or, if you want more privacy…" He looked around.

She gave him a half-hearted smile. "I wonder if Della has any bear claws left."

Shane grinned. "There's only one way to find out."

They walked over to the café, and once they were seated with their coffees and pastries, Shane looked at her. "Your comments about the authorities make me think there's something terribly wrong. I want to understand. Not just for our working relationship, but because you're part of this community. You shouldn't live in fear of the situation with your son. But if people don't understand, they will call in the authorities. I want to help you. Helen would want me to help you."

Leah took a deep breath as she picked at her pastry. She'd hoped that the sweetness would make the conversation easier, but it only made her feel nauseated.

"Their father was a drug addict. For a long time, I didn't realize it, because it started out as a painkiller addiction. He'd been injured in a skiing accident and had legitimate pain. However, over time, it turned into an addiction, which made him use worse drugs to get the same relief."

Looking back, she wished she'd understood the signs of drug addiction. People wondered why she didn't trust others. Maybe it was because of all the times the man she thought she could trust looked her in the eyes and lied.

She took a sip of her coffee. "He ended up losing his job because of his addiction, so I worked while he watched the kids. However, being a father was too much for him. Especially with his need for the drugs. When Dylan misbehaved, he would physically harm him. I didn't know. He would explain away Dylan's injuries as being normal kid stuff. I had no reason to doubt my husband, and Dylan always agreed with his father's story."

Even now as she opened up to Shane, she tried to think back to anything that would have clued her in sooner. How could she have protected the boys better?

"I'm sorry," he said. "That must have been difficult for you. What did you do?"

The sympathy on his face made her want to trust him. But how many times had she fallen for that same look from others? She looked Shane directly in the eye. "The first time, I believed him when he said he accidentally took too much. But something about it didn't feel right, so I was more watchful. By the time I figured out my husband had a problem, I was pregnant with Ryan, doing the best I could to take care of Dylan, hold down a job and deal with my husband's drug addiction."

"Why didn't you leave him?"

Leah sighed. It was so easy for people to judge her situation and her marriage and make it as simple as that.

"Where would we have gone? Even though it sounds like everything was horrible, he tried to get clean. Things were only bad when he relapsed. I always thought that if I tried harder, worked harder and did more, he would beat it. Before the drugs, he was a good man. He helped put Erin and Nicole through college. He was there for us when no one else was. I couldn't abandon him."

Remembering the good times made her feel disloyal for speaking against him. Yes, he had had his faults, but to completely paint him a monster wasn't an accurate depiction. At his best, he was a great father. At his worst...

"I struggle with how much I trusted him. Especially with the boys. I never imagined that their father would have hurt them. Once I found out, he was never alone with the boys. But the damage had been done."

The look on Shane's face made her feel even worse. No matter how many times she'd been assured she'd done the best she could under the circumstances, people on the outside couldn't understand how hard she'd tried to keep it together for the kids and how much therapy her family had been through.

But even what she'd told him seemed like too much.

"I'm sorry," she said. "That's a lot to dump on you. Too much to explain, except to say that I spent years trying to do the right thing by my family. Unfortunately, because of the circumstances with his father, Dylan learned some inappropriate behaviors. We were in counseling when we lived in Denver, but the program lost its funding, and I couldn't afford to pay for it on my own. Having income wouldn't just help me pay my way with my sisters, but it would give me the ability to put Dylan back in counseling."

Shane looked thoughtful, like he was trying to understand but couldn't quite figure out what to make of her troubled little boy.

"I know it's tempting to want a shortcut," he said slowly. "But you need to understand, if you buy those cows and something goes wrong, any rancher would have a hard time climbing out of it."

Once again, they were back to this. She supposed she could understand his desire to want to keep her from being hurt. But is this what he would advise a fellow rancher? Someone with years of experience?

He leaned forward. "I appreciate you wanting to pull your own weight. I meant what I said earlier about helping you. If you're as fast a learner as you say you are, you'll have what you need by fall."

She only half listened as he outlined the job, responsibilities and payment. She could do any work. It wasn't that she was afraid of hard work or that she didn't want to do a particular job. He named his wage and it was a fair one, and that was all that mattered.

"I accept," she said. "I'm eager to learn about ranching. I know I won't find a better deal, and the terms you're offering sound fair."

He looked relieved as he sat back against the chair, like maybe she was doing him a bigger favor than she'd thought. Maybe she'd underestimated him as a man. Once again, she couldn't help thinking that she'd put him in a box that he didn't belong in.

* * *

When they'd finished their coffee, Shane had Leah follow him back to his ranch so he could show her around. At least she was starting to show signs of having trust. He wanted to give her the benefit of the doubt, and he was trying to give her time to come around. But every time he thought she was opening up, the guarded expression returned to her face, and something changed between them. How long would this détente last?

He'd like to do more to help her, but he was like every other rancher in town. Money was tight, and they were all doing the best they could with what they had. In a way, that's what Leah was doing. When they pulled up to his barn, he got out of the truck and went to open Leah's door. But by the time he got there, she was already stepping out of her car.

"Why are you people so eager to rush to open other people's doors?"

He sighed. She really didn't understand the life out here.

"Because it's what we do," he said. He could see the confusion on her face, and he wasn't sure how to make her feel better. He'd hoped that in her time here, she would have started to learn that people were here to help each other.

"The reason we're here on this earth is to look out for each other. I can understand why you'd be afraid. It sounds like you've been hurt a lot. But I'm here to help you. Helen loved you. Every time I talked to her, all I heard was how much she loved you and your sisters. You three were everything to her. Helen was like family to me. How can I not help you?"

She still looked suspicious of him. "I understand that you think you're doing it for Helen. But why is everyone else so nice to us? What do they have to gain?"

He thought about her questions for a moment, wondering how she could have gotten so hurt in life that she would make so many assumptions about him. About the world. She might be going to their church, but she clearly didn't know God.

"Didn't you understand the sermon on Sunday? Pastor Jeff talked about loving our neighbors. You're our neighbor. Of course we would love you."

"I've been to enough churches to know that loving your neighbor is just an excuse for prying into their business."

The familiar defensive stance returned to her body, like she was once again readying for a fight. "One of my church neighbors reported us to social services. Yes, Dylan had a huge bruise on his face. But that one was legitimately gained by his own stupidity. He'd been at the playground with some other kids and was running and didn't notice that he'd gotten too close to the swings. Another kid hit him, and bam! Giant bruise on the face."

He couldn't help smiling at her motion as she recreated the scene. Knowing kids, he could definitely see it happening. Only Leah wasn't smiling.

"Our lives were turned upside down for months. The irony of it was that it was during one of Jason's sober periods, so when they investigated, they found nothing wrong."

The pain in her voice was evident. He wished he

could do something to make her feel better. But she wasn't through.

"The stress of the investigation made Jason relapse for the final time. We hadn't done anything wrong, but it led to a lot of bad things. One of them was that Dylan learned that threatening to call child services was often enough to get him what he wanted."

She shook her head slowly. He couldn't imagine how hard that must have been.

"The church people were fast enough to call the authorities, but not one of them were there when I tried getting help for my husband. Or when he died."

Ouch. He couldn't explain their behavior, but he hated that they had left such a sour taste in her mouth. Hopefully, being here would help her see the church in a new light.

"Not all Christians are like that. I'm sorry you had a bad experience. You'll find that the friendship and help-fulness you're receiving in this community is genuine."

She lifted her chin with a challenging stare. "So even Harold has my best interests in mind?"

She had to bring that up, didn't she? "I don't think Harold is trying to hurt you. I'm sure he believes that everything will be all right with his cattle. He doesn't have much experience as a rancher. He hired a ranch manager who took care of all that for him. But his ranch manager moved on, leaving Harold to take care of things himself. That's when I noticed things starting to go downhill with his operation. If it were a more experienced rancher taking on his herd, I wouldn't be as concerned. Most of us understand the essentials of biosecurity and how to keep our herd safe."

Instead of making her feel better, his words seemed

to have the opposite effect. She looked almost angry. "Would you take them on?"

He shrugged. "If I had more time and more money, maybe. But I'm a small operation, and I don't have the resources others do. It would take everything I have to add his cows to my herd, and that's too much of a risk for me to bear."

She nodded slowly, like she understood, so he continued. "That's why I advised you not to buy those cows. If it's a risk I can't take, I would never ask you to do the same. If I thought there was even the slightest chance that things would work out for you, I would help."

Leah let out a long sigh. She still didn't seem like she was going to give up on the idea, but he'd done everything he could to try to convince her.

"I don't know who to trust," she finally said.

That was the real issue. The one they'd touched on with her past. She'd been hurt so many times; believing that he had her best interests in mind was a challenge. How could he convince her? This wasn't about him, but the pain she carried.

"Sometimes you have to have a little faith and be willing to trust in others," he said. "I know it's hard, but the people of Columbine Springs are good people. Our church is a good church. And our God far surpasses them all in goodness. I don't know how else to communicate that to you, but I hope that, in time, you will learn to trust in that goodness."

Of course, that wasn't the whole story. He didn't want her getting overblown expectations. "That's not to say that everyone here is perfect. You'll find people you don't rub well with. You might even have someone do you a wrong turn. But it's what you do with it that matters. Even Jesus knew the pain of having a friend betray Him. God doesn't promise us a pain-free life by following Him, but I believe that life with Him is far better than life without it."

Though Leah still looked doubtful, she nodded. "I know that was the message at church on Sunday, but you have to understand. Everyone in my life has always let me down. The only people I've ever been able to count on are my sisters."

"Humans are fallible," he said. "We do our best, but we're all going to mess up from time to time. That's why we need God. That's why Jesus's work was so important. Without Him, we wouldn't be able to know the depth of God's love the way we do."

She nodded again, and some of the weariness left her face. Maybe they were making progress after all.

"Others have been looking out for you, as well. Sometimes we don't always see it, and it takes years to understand. But think about Helen, and what she did for you. Ten years ago, it would never have seemed possible."

A sad look crossed her face, and he regretted having said something.

"I wish she had come back into our lives ten years ago. I would have liked to have had a relationship with her."

"She was a good woman. The best I ever knew. I'm sorry you didn't have the chance to know her, but I hope you know how much she loved you."

She nodded slowly. "I used to hate her for leaving us with him. But I didn't realize the difficulty in navigating the system. Now, I have a deeper love and understanding for her, because I know how hard it is to deal with so much difficulty."

Based on what he'd learned so far, hers had not been an easy life.

"I understand things weren't good with your father."

She shook her head. "No, and there wasn't anything Helen could have done about it. We didn't even refer to him as our father. We called him the Colonel. When he died, we were all presented with letters, accounting for everything he'd done for us. All dollars and cents."

She slowly shook her head again, as if to dispel the memory. "That's when I realized that all the things we thought were our fault growing up were actually his. I would do anything for my boys. I've worked a lot of demeaning jobs to keep a roof over their heads and food on the table. My children are worth it to me. The fact that we weren't worth anything to our father— that's a defect in him, not us."

He shouldn't have been surprised by her wisdom, but, from the tiny lines on her face, he could see that it had been hard earned.

The wind kicked up and blew loose strands of her dark hair around her face. She brushed it aside and turned in the direction of the wind, shielding her eyes from the sun.

She had a depth of intelligence that he respected. He liked that about her. Actually, he liked a lot of things about her. At times like these, he thought she was the kind of person he'd ask out on a date. When they weren't fighting about stupid things, he liked hearing what she had to say. Once again, he thought about Gina and how wrong he'd been in pursuing her.

After hearing Leah's story, he knew she had the strength in her that Gina never had. Gina had always been quick to complain about how Natalie's father had left them, leaving her without any support. She'd blamed everyone else for her problems, unwilling to take responsibility for the things that had gone wrong in her life.

Leah was different.

Maybe he was still in rescue mode, but he really wished there was more he could do for her family than give her a job. Leah wasn't expecting everyone to take care of everything for her, to make her life better. She knew how to do it for herself. He admired that can-do spirit, and he wanted to participate in it. Not so much as a rescuer but as a partner and a friend.

But as they walked over to the barn and she greeted the horses with such warmth, he, not for the first time, felt the pull of wanting to be more than friends. He hadn't felt that since Gina left, and now he wanted...

He had to stop thinking of her this way. Especially if she was going to be working for him. He didn't want to take advantage of her or make her feel obligated to get involved with him. If whatever was between them was meant to be, it would work itself out in due time.

He turned to her. "Let me continue with the tour, and I'll explain the things I need from you. It won't be exciting, and it will be a lot of dirty work."

Looking her up and down, he noted that she was dressed for a job interview, not a hard day at the ranch. "Wear clothes you don't mind getting dirty, wet, ripped or ruined. If I were you, I'd make use of the thrift store in town and pick up some old boots."

She smiled at him, another warm expression that

made him wonder what he'd ever seen in Gina. "We did that before we got here."

Once again, he had to give her an A for enthusiasm.

He gestured at his ATV. "Nowadays, this is what most of us use to check on stock and feed. I also use it to ride down to the ditch and turn my water off and on. People think the cowboy lifestyle is all about the horses, and while they still have a place on the ranch, a lot of times this is more convenient."

The expression on her face told him that was one thing she hadn't considered about ranching. This was a good time to give her a lesson.

"Even on a ranch as small as yours, a lot of times your cattle are going to be miles away. From your house to the far end, it's a good two miles. If you have to check on your animals or supplement their feed, how are you going to get there?"

Leah bit her lip. "I guess I thought I'd walk, but that's not very practical, is it?"

Shane gestured to a bale of hay. "Pick it up."

When she did, she struggled at the weight of it. As he knew she would. "Take it over there to the end of the barn, by that stall."

As she struggled to carry the hay across the barn, he said, "Now imagine yourself carrying that a mile. Could you do it?"

A few weeks working with him and she would be lifting and throwing bales of hay like they were nothing. But even he wasn't stupid enough to carry it a mile.

When she was finished, she put her hands on her hips and heaved in deep breaths. "I guess I need a pickup truck or something. I know this gets easier with practice, but wow. You must think I'm really stupid for not thinking about things like this."

He walked over to the refrigerator he kept in the barn and grabbed a bottle of water. Then he tossed it over to her. "Not stupid. Inexperienced. I have no doubt that after a few months of working with me, you'll have a better sense of what it takes to run a ranch. You'll have learned all the practical things that you hadn't considered before. It's not rocket science. It just comes from experience. I know you think I've been hard on you and I keep discouraging you, but I don't want you to fail simply because you haven't thought everything through."

As she drank the water, she nodded. But the wariness had returned to her eyes.

"You're smart and capable," he continued. "You have more grit and gumption then a lot of people I know. I understand why you don't trust easily. But I'm asking you to have a little faith in the fact that I'm here to help you. I made a promise to Helen, and I'm doing for you what Helen always wanted to do."

She brushed the hay off her pants. Then she looked up at him. "I've given you more trust than I've given anyone else in a long time. Don't make me regret it."

She finished her water and tossed the empty bottle into the recycling bin. "Now, what else do you need me to do? I've got about an hour before I need to get home and start dinner."

And just like that, they were back to business. A good thing, since he didn't want to think about trust issues…or the fact that he liked the way she fit right in at his ranch a little too much.

* * *

After the boys were in bed, Leah brewed some tea and brought it into the family room, where she and her sisters often spent their evenings.

Once they were settled, she explained the events of the day.

"So this guy wants to sell us his herd at a ridiculously low price?" Erin asked, setting down the book she'd been reading.

Leah nodded. "It's almost too good to be true, and I guess it is, since the herd has been exposed to a disease that could prove to be quite expensive," she said.

Nicole gestured at the book she'd been reading. "It's really fascinating if you study more about it. There's a whole chapter devoted to it in this book. How long ago did you say the last cow tested positive?"

"A couple of months ago. Harold says that everything should be fine, but Shane says it could be up to a year before they know for sure that the entire herd is clean, so I don't know what to think. But after being at Shane's today and learning how his ranch operates, I can see where we do have a lot to learn. Maybe it's better that we wait."

Erin and Nicole looked at each other. Then Nicole said, "Are you sure you don't like him? Everything's been Shane says this and Shane says that. You're not letting your feelings for him cloud your judgment, are you?"

Leah sighed. She hated how well her sisters knew her. Especially because she wasn't sure Nicole was wrong. She did like Shane. Maybe a little too much. Sometimes the way he smiled at her made her feel all giddy inside, like a teenager. But she couldn't allow these feelings to take over rational thinking. Not when she had a family to provide for.

"I don't know," she said honestly. "However, I do know that Shane is right about us not being ready to run the ranch. When he described his operation to me and gave me my list of duties, I realized how much more we have to learn. Even simple things, like how do we get food to the cattle, and the water? Shane has machines and equipment to do all that for him, but we have nothing. We don't even own a pickup truck."

Her sisters looked at each other again, like they still thought her hesitance was more about her feelings for Shane than her practicality.

"You have a point," Erin said. "I came to the same conclusion myself. I was talking to my boss, and he has a bunch of equipment he doesn't use. He wants to turn the barn into an event space, which means that he's got to store the equipment elsewhere or get rid of it. He's leaning toward getting rid of it, but because it's so old and worn, he doesn't know anyone around here who would buy it."

"Except us," Nicole said. "Right?"

Erin nodded. "Exactly. I mentioned that we might be able to use it. He thought that was a great idea. There's nothing wrong with any of it, because he takes very good care of his things. It's just old, and a lot of the ranchers around here have all upgraded. He's willing to sell it to me for a good price. I told him I would discuss it with you guys first. So here I am, saying I think we should do it."

Leah knew the expression on her sister's face. She was in take-no-prisoners mode, and she'd already made up her mind. As Erin continued explaining the deal, Leah had to agree with her sister. It was a great opportunity. But even as her sisters' excitement grew, Leah couldn't help feeling more disconcerted. She'd spent only a day at Shane's ranch, and already she knew they were getting in way over their heads.

"This sounds great," Nicole said. "I was saving this for a rainy day, but this seems like a good time to share. I've been selling off the things from my wedding, and a few women got into a bidding war over my wedding dress. I actually have quite a bit of money to contribute."

Erin's grin couldn't possibly be any bigger. "An opportunity like this happens once in a lifetime. I say we get the cows."

"I agree," Nicole said. "So we're going for it?"

At Erin's enthusiastic yes, Leah couldn't bring herself to say no. But she couldn't agree either, so she didn't say anything.

Both of her sisters looked so excited, so happy. Only it made the sick feeling in her stomach grow worse. While her sisters were enthusiastically discussing finances and what they could contribute, Leah had nothing. True, she had a job now, so she could help with household expenses. But she had nothing to give to the start-up cost.

"I don't really have anything to contribute," Leah said, sighing. She'd have liked to have reminded them of Shane's misgivings, but the last thing she needed were more questions about her feelings for him.

Erin smiled at her. "But that's the point. With the great deals we're getting, plus Nicole's money, you don't have to contribute anything. This is the best news ever. I know you're worried about finances, but we have enough so that you don't need to. It's time for us all to start living."

Easy for her to say. She was bringing significantly more to the table.

As her sisters continued making plans, Leah told herself that at least she would be pitching in by learning the ropes at Shane's ranch. Her new job would not only give her money for the household expenses but give her practical knowledge on how to make the ranch run more effectively.

Still, it didn't feel like enough.

When her sisters gave her room to talk, Leah asked, "So, what do I tell Shane about leasing the land? He told me that he was only going to lease part of it for the summer, leaving the rest for us to have when we get cattle in the fall. Do you think that land will be enough?"

"That's a great idea," Erin said. "It'll give us another revenue stream, so we can look at other things we want for the ranch. I feel bad that we still haven't achieved Nicole's dream of getting all the animals she wants. At the very least, we need a few horses."

Nicole nodded. "Definitely. Not only am I dying for horses for my sake, but I've been reading a lot about equine therapy and how it helps children with behavioral issues. The boys are so fascinated by horses. I want them to have exposure to that."

Leah tried not to be too offended at the way her sister was taking over her sons' care. She knew Nicole meant well and that Nicole wasn't just getting this information for the sake of her boys, but because she genuinely liked working with children and wanted to learn about all the different ways she could help them.

Fortunately, that was another way Leah would be taking care of her own future.

"Shane is going to let me bring the boys to work. He said it will be good for them to learn different chores that they will eventually do at our place."

Erin stood. "I'm glad to hear it. And now, since we are getting some cows, some ranch equipment and maybe even some horses, it's time we break out the secret stash of celebratory chocolate I've been hiding. We deserve a little treat."

As Erin walked out of the room, Leah heard a noise from the hallway. She turned and saw Dylan, hiding around the corner.

She turned to him. "What are you doing out of bed? You know the rules."

Instead of looking offended that he'd been caught in the act, Dylan smiled. "We're getting cows? And horses?"

Great. He'd overheard everything. What happened if it didn't work out? The boys would be disappointed, and she hated having to manage the disappointments. They'd had so many in their short lives already.

Nicole stood. "We sure are. But you know what happens to little boys who don't follow the rules. If you're going to enjoy our new animals, you've got to get your sleep."

Dylan let out an excited whoop, then turned and ran back to his room. While Leah was grateful that her son could be so easily appeased, she also couldn't help worrying. Nicole seemed to sense her thoughts.

"It'll be fine. No one's going to take the ranch out from under us. You don't always have to brace yourself for the worst-case scenarios. Sometimes, good things are just good things, and you're allowed to celebrate."

Optimism was a luxury Leah didn't have right now. She had to hope that, somehow, everything would work out in the end. And it wouldn't hurt to say a prayer, too.

As she closed her eyes to try to come up with something that sounded intelligent enough for God to listen to, she thought about what Shane said earlier today. That just because she believed in God and trusted in Him, it didn't mean that everything was going to work out for her perfectly. But she liked what Shane had said about not going it alone. As she settled in her chair, she bumped the table beside it and heard something fall. She turned and looked to see what she'd knocked over. A book lay wedged between the table and the wall. Leah reached for it.

Funny, she hadn't noticed it before. Though they'd cleaned this room well, she'd missed it. Based on the way everything sat, somehow this book must have gotten wedged in the chair and loosened when she'd knocked the chair against the table. As she looked at the book, her chest felt heavy and her eyes filled with tears.

The Bible.

And when she opened it, she knew it wasn't just a Bible, but Helen's Bible. Well-loved and worn, filled with highlights and notes and little pieces of paper stuck here and there, this wasn't just a book. It was a treasure.

And though she hadn't given herself to such moments of fancy very often, she couldn't help thinking that perhaps this was God's way of answering her prayers. Letting her know that, even with all these ups and downs and moments of confusion, He was still there, watching out for her.

Chapter Seven

Even though Shane had given himself a stern talking to before Leah's arrival about not getting attached, his heart did a funny little leap as her car pulled into his driveway. Dylan bounded out as Leah went around to unbuckle his brother. While Leah was busy with Ryan, Dylan ran to him and threw his arms around him in a big hug.

"Mister Shane! I've missed you."

There was no way he could remain unattached to this little boy who clung to him like he was starving for attention. He knew that wasn't true, because he'd seen Leah and her sisters with the boys and knew how much they loved them. But as Shane swung Dylan up into his arms, he realized that he was the only man these boys had. How often had this boy gotten a loving touch from a man? He gave Dylan a final squeeze, then set him down.

"Are you ready for your cowboy lessons, partner?"

Dylan nodded. "I am. My mom says that I have to be good today. And—" he pulled something out of his pocket "—I made this for you. I'm supposed to tell you I'm sorry for throwing a fit and breaking your mug."

Dylan handed him a drawing. Once again, Shane's heart made a funny little leap. It was a picture of a family. A mom, a dad and two boys. All riding a giant horse.

"That's you, my mom, me and my brother. We're going for a horse ride. Mom says that if we're good, and we learn all the rules and we ask you really nice, maybe you'll let us spend some time with your horse." A sly smile filled the little boy's face. "And I'm hoping you might finally let us ride your horse."

Of course Dylan wasn't thinking of them in terms of being a family. Why was Shane foolish enough to let his mind go there? He was almost as obsessed with the idea of having a family as Leah seemed to be with her ranch. He just hoped that, as he'd been able to convince Leah of her foolishness in taking that path right now, he could convince his heart that this wasn't the right time to be getting mixed up with Leah and her boys.

Leah approached, holding Ryan's hand. "Good morning," she said, giving him a smile he wouldn't mind waking up to every morning.

Could he be any more pathetic? Hadn't he just told himself not to do this?

"Good morning. Dylan made me a nice picture, and I accept his apology."

He refolded the picture and put it in his shirt pocket. "At lunch, we'll go inside and hang it on my fridge. But for right now, we've got to go make sure that my cows have enough water."

He gestured toward his pickup and turned to Leah.

"I hope your car seat is easy to move in and out of the different vehicles."

She nodded. "It's no trouble at all." As Leah went to get everything situated for Ryan, Shane turned to the boys. "I'm glad you came to help. I'll try to explain everything to you, and we'll go over the rules as we ride to the cows. But the most important thing to remember is that you always need to stay where I can see you, and you shouldn't touch anything without asking."

Dylan nodded enthusiastically. "That's what Mom told us this morning. She said it's just like at the house. If we see a snake, we can't pick it up. We have to ask for a grown-up to help."

Shane couldn't help laughing at Dylan's visible disgust at having to seek an adult's help. Dylan was all boy, and that was probably part of the problem. Not that boys couldn't be raised by women, but, sometimes, they needed someone who could understand things like their fascination with snakes.

"And she's absolutely right. Some of the snakes here are harmless. But some snakes, like rattlers, they can kill you."

Dylan groaned. "I know. Aunt Nicole always tells us that. She used to have a pet snake. We got to play with it. But she says the snakes that live here aren't like those snakes, and they aren't to be petted or picked up."

The way Dylan said it, it was clear the little boy had been given that lecture multiple times. Shane had to give himself a mental kick for thinking that just because they were women, they wouldn't understand certain things. Nicole having a pet snake surprised him, but in a way, he was glad to hear it. The sisters were unlike any group of women he'd ever met, and while he'd been thinking that they had much to learn from him, he realized he could probably learn just as much from them.

"Your aunt is absolutely right," Shane said. "The longer you're out here, the more you'll learn about snakes and other wildlife."

Dylan nodded. "That's what my mom says. My aunts think it's a good idea for us to learn about your cows for when our cows come."

He hadn't expected them to teach the boys to look so far in advance, but it was good. It was nice getting them thinking about the future, because so few people did.

"It'll definitely be good. But you won't be getting cows for a while."

Dylan shook his head. His face scrunched up into a scowl, like the ones he got just before throwing a fit. What had he said wrong this time?

"We're getting cows soon. Aunt Erin said so. She's buying a tractor from Mister Ricky. And my mom is getting cows from one of her friends."

He took a deep breath. Tried to process what the little boy had just said. They were getting cows from her mom's friend? Not Harold's cows?

Leah rejoined them, smiling. "All set. Anything else you need?"

Shane turned and looked at her. "We're good. Boys, climb into the back seat of the truck."

As the boys scampered off, he turned and looked at Leah. "Dylan says you're getting cows. Did you find some other herd? I'm happy to take a look at them so you know you're not getting into something you can't handle."

He tried to keep his words casual, when what he wanted to do was ask her how she could be so stupid as to not heed his warnings.

Leah sighed. "I told my sisters about Harold's latest offer, and they felt it was one we can't refuse. With Erin working at Ricky's, she learned he was selling a bunch of his equipment for cheap. And she knew that the price Harold offered on his cattle was too good to pass up. I got outvoted."

She might have been outvoted, but judging by the boys' excitement and her rather bland way of telling him, she didn't seem too put out by it.

"Do they understand the risk that you're taking in getting those cows? Do they even understand what Bangs is?"

Leah nodded. "Oddly enough, Nicole has been reading a book about animal disease. She thinks this herd will be manageable."

There she went with that crazy reliance on books again. It wasn't that Shane had any problems with books. But there were some things about ranching you couldn't learn by reading a book. You had to live it—experience it—to understand it.

"And where are you going to keep them? I thought we agreed on my land lease."

Leah nodded. "You can still lease that land. We'll put them in the other pasture, the one you said we would use for our herd when we got it."

Her words only proved that they were not ready to run a ranch on their own. "If you run a herd on both pastures, one isn't going to have time to regrow and develop for next year. That's why you alternate pastures. While one is being used, the other has a chance to grow. If you run too many cattle on your land, it gets all eaten up, and then you have to supplement."

Her expression told him that she hadn't considered that, and he was glad. Perhaps it wasn't too late to end this madness.

"I didn't realize that," she said. "I mean, yes, I've read about rotating pastures. But I guess I hadn't realized why."

"That's why I wanted you to spend some time helping me run my ranch. So you could learn. So that things you read in books make sense in a practical way. In theory, biosafety practices sound easy. But have you considered how you will keep your herd from infecting my herd when you go between the two?"

The blank expression on her face told him she had no idea what he was talking about.

"Let's say, in the morning, you check on your cattle. Once you get done checking your herd, you will have to completely change clothing, including your shoes, before you come to my house. If you use one of your vehicles to go check on your herd, you can't bring it to my house. Everything that touches your herd must be completely sanitized before it can come near me or my herd. And when I come visit you, I have to be aware of the same sanitary practices."

She looked like she was thinking about his words. "I didn't realize that it was so serious. From what I read, the bacteria just has to be exposed to the air for a few hours and it dies," she said.

He nodded. "Here's the trouble. Let's say I step in manure from an infected animal. It gets on my boot.

I go back to my place. The stuff from my boot comes off in my pasture, and my cow eats it. My cow is now infected."

Leah stared at him. "Your cow would eat it?"

"Or my dogs. Cow dung is a dog's favorite treat."

She looked puzzled. "So, if your dog comes to my house and eats something, he could get it?"

"That's why this is such a dangerous disease. It's easily transmitted between a variety of different species, including humans. Did your book tell you that your sons could get it?"

He turned to look at the boys, who were getting impatient in the back of his truck. Almost as if to prove his point, Ryan was picking his nose.

"Look at Ryan. He's picking his nose and eating it. What if he had just touched something that was infected? He's now stuck it up his nose and into his mouth."

Leah's face turned white. He was pretty sure he'd proven his point.

He gestured to his truck. "I realize that as your employer, I can't tell you what to do with your personal life. However, I do want to make it clear that if you get those cows, we're going to put in some very strict rules about biosecurity."

She stared at him for a moment. "You're not going to fire me?"

No one would fault him for it. But if he let her go, the women would be stumbling about in even more ignorance. With his lesson right now, he'd been able to impress upon Leah the seriousness of her actions. The seriousness of biosecurity. Continuing to work with her was a safe and practical way to show her more of what she needed to know.

He shook his head. "No. I need help, and you need lessons. And it's as you said. You got outvoted. But, out of curiosity, has your sister told Ricky about the cows you're getting? You make sure she does and lets him know all the details. He may want to put in some rules for the biosecurity of his own herd."

The concern on her face made him hopeful that she would rethink her decision. But was it enough to convince her sisters?

As they drove out to his cows to water them, Shane tried working out how he would explain things to the other sisters. But what baggage did they have that would make it hard for them to trust his word?

Based on Helen's stories, it wasn't just Leah who'd come from a bad place.

Maybe it was time to stop trying to convince them and find another solution.

Tending the cows always brought him a lot of peace. Even with the distraction of a pretty lady and her rambunctious boys, it gave him the chance to chew on an idea. By the time Leah and the kids left, Shane knew what he had to do.

Leah wasn't going to like it, and he didn't much like it, either. But someone had to buy those cows before she made a terrible mistake.

When Leah and the boys left for the day, he called Harold and made arrangements to buy the cows. Poor Leah thought Harold was just trying to be nice, selling them the cows at a good price, but Shane had managed to talk him down even further.

That still left the problem of where to keep the herd. But Shane had an idea he hoped would work.

Shane entered the café and walked to the table where he knew fellow rancher Larry Mathieson would be sitting. Larry always spent Tuesdays at the café, having a cup of coffee and pastry in honor of his beloved Myra, who'd passed over a year ago.

Before Shane got to the table, Larry stood. "Shane. Just thinking about you. I hope you'll join me for a cup of coffee."

At least now he didn't feel so bad. But why had Larry been thinking about him? Before Shane could sit, Larry waved at Della and said, "Get Shane here a cup of coffee and one of them bear claws."

Then Larry turned to him and let out a long sigh. "My daughter has been bugging me to leave the ranch and move to Denver. I just don't know if I can take the city life. But it's also lonesome here without Myra."

The old man's eyes filled with tears, and Shane wondered what it must be like to lose the love of your life like that. To have loved and been loved so deeply that you are struggling with living now that the person was gone. He hadn't felt that way when Gina had left; instead he'd been mostly sad at losing Natalie and disappointed that his only chance of a relationship had ended.

He liked Leah. Sometimes he thought he more than liked her. But was he setting himself up for failure when she found ranch life too difficult? If his plan came to fruition and she found out, she was bound to hate him. But would she forgive him when she realized what he'd saved her from?

He was willing to risk losing her if it meant saving her from ruin.

"What does your going to Denver have to do with me?" Shane asked.

Larry cleared his throat. "I was hoping you would look after things for me. Watch my place. Tend the few animals I have left."

Shane nodded. "Of course. I was always happy to watch your ranch when you and Myra went on vacation, and you had a lot more stock back then. This will be no trouble at all."

And him doing Larry a favor made it a little easier to ask Larry the favor he'd been seeking him out for.

"Truth be told, I'm here to ask for your help. You know those cows Harold is trying to unload?"

Larry made a noise. "Don't tell me some fool has agreed to buy them. I don't have a herd anymore, but if the wrong fellow buys those cattle and they're infected, upstream from the wrong ranch, it could devastate this community."

Shane nodded. "Exactly what I was thinking. I don't know if you've met the women who inherited Helen's ranch or not, but they're eager to buy those cows."

Larry looked disgusted. "Someone's got to talk them out of that. Where they're located, if the rest of the herd ends up with it, it could easily spread to neighboring ranches. Do those women have any idea what they're doing?"

The old man's opposition to their plan made Shane feel a little bit better about what he was going to do. Or at least hoped to do, with Larry's help.

"I've tried explaining, but they believe Harold's

optimistic view that, since it hasn't turned up in any more of his cattle, his herd is disease-free."

"Fool. He never did have a lick of sense, and I can't believe those women are under his influence. What do you want me to do about it?"

Shane took a deep breath. "I'm going to buy the herd. The trouble is, I don't have a place to keep them, and I was thinking about that south pasture of yours. It's far enough away from any neighboring ranches since it borders on national forestland, and you don't have any water going through it."

Larry nodded slowly. "It's definitely an isolated spot. But can you afford to take on such a burden?"

Shane shook his head. "No. But I don't think this community can take on the burden of any more cows getting sick. If this thing spreads, a lot of good families will lose their livelihoods. I know the sisters mean well, and they're desperate. If they won't listen to reason, I've got to find another way to stop them."

Larry leaned back in his chair. "And you knew my land was available. I won't be running cows on it for a while, maybe not ever. It's a great place to quarantine the animals."

Shane nodded. "I hope you'll give me a good price on the lease. I'm already paying them more than I paid Helen for their land. But I know they need it, so I'm trying to do right by them."

Larry chuckled as he shook his head. "You're doing us all a big favor by isolating those cows. I've no use for the land right now, and since this is just you doing your part to help your neighbors, I can't accept money for it. Besides, you're already helping me out by looking after my place."

He felt like a heel for what he was doing, but he was running out of options. Even though he'd thought he'd talked some sense into Leah, she also seemed to be just as easily talked out of it.

With arrangements made for the land, Shane went to pick up the cows. On his way to Harold's place, he stopped by John Hansen's to see if he was free. It would be helpful to have the vet with him to give him some idea of what he was getting into.

Harold didn't have the best of land even in a good year. But with the lack of rain in recent months, the land wasn't enough to feed the herd. The cattle needed hay, and it was obvious they hadn't been getting any. Bone thin and so close to starvation, if there was a disease running rampant through the herd, they would easily fall prey in their weakened state.

John didn't need long to examine the cattle. "Are you sure you want to take this herd on? Harold never used my services, so I don't know their history, but I can tell you already that they are going to need a lot more TLC than a normal herd."

Shane nodded. "I was afraid you were going to say that. But I don't know that I have much of a choice." He'd already explained to John about the sisters and their determination to raise the cows.

"I don't know why you're so set on helping. You say you're doing it for Helen, but even Helen thought you can't fix stupid. Maybe this is something they need to learn on their own."

Shane let out a long sigh. He'd made a lot of mistakes in his early years of ranching, and no one had been there to save him. But he'd learned from the experiences, and he'd like to think that's why he was doing so well now. An inexperienced rancher getting these cows wasn't just one mistake. There could be mistakes that would be devastating to everyone. "I know. But those two boys of hers…"

John nodded. "You always had a soft spot for children. I just hope your heart doesn't get broken this time."

The trouble with living in a small town and being involved in the men's group, sharing prayer requests, sharing your life, is that sometimes people knew too much about your business for comfort. Everyone here knew about Gina.

Was he once again making a fool of himself over a woman with kids?

"I don't know what else to do," he said, looking over at his friend. "And it isn't just about the boys. It's about the fact that these women don't know what they're doing, and they know nothing about bio-security. How do we keep them from infecting every other herd in the area?"

John nodded. "I didn't think of that." He looked around at Harold's ranch. "We're fortunate that none of the cows are dead yet. I think that might have been his plan, just letting them die out here."

Then John spat on the ground. "Makes me sick. No animal should die like that. I suppose you're right. I wouldn't want an inexperienced rancher taking them on. At least you have the know-how. I know you haven't asked, but I'll give you a break on my fees. It's the least I can do, because you're right. A herd in this state presents a very real threat to our community."

For a moment, Shane's chest felt heavy. He hadn't asked, but to save money on vet fees would indeed be a blessing. With buying the cows and paying Leah, it was taking everything he had. In the long run, he knew it was the right decision, but in the short run, things were going to be tight.

He just prayed that Leah would find it in her heart to understand.

After a long week working with Shane, Leah's sisters had insisted that she take all of Saturday off and spend the day doing something fun with the boys. Erin had even pressed a twenty into Leah's hand and told her not to come home until it was gone.

Frankly, Leah had been too exhausted to argue.

Which was how she'd ended up at B.J.'s, a little place shaped like an ice cream cone on the edge of town. According to Shane, it was the place to go on a hot summer's day, and it seemed, as she arrived, he'd taken his own advice.

Shane was already there, enjoying a cone like he didn't have a care in the world.

Before she could decide about whether or not to approach him, Dylan ran toward him. "Mister Shane!"

The poor guy probably needed a day off just as much as she did, and here they were, bothering him.

But Shane smiled as her son barreled into him, knocking the ice cream right out of his hands.

Dylan jerked away and started to cry. "It was an accident. I didn't mean to. Please don't be mad. Please don't hurt me."

"I'm not going to hurt you. I've never hurt anyone in my life. It's just ice cream. Come here."

Shane took the little boy into his arms and gave him

a big hug. "It was an accident. Accidents happen. Did I hurt you when you broke my mug?"

Maybe that was a bad example, considering Dylan had accused him of doing so, but Dylan shook his head. Then Dylan burrowed closer to him. "My dad used to hurt me sometimes."

Leah's heart dipped at her son's words. It had taken months of therapy for Dylan to make that admission previously. Clearly, her son trusted Shane more deeply than she'd thought.

"I'm sorry to hear that," he said, giving the boy a hard, tight squeeze. "But I'm not like your dad, and I will never hurt you."

Dylan burrowed himself in closer, squeezing him tighter. "Maybe now that he's gone, you could be my dad instead."

A lump formed in Leah's throat, and she wasn't sure how to respond.

Shane gave him another squeeze. "It's not that simple. But I'll always be here for you as your friend."

Some of the tension she'd been holding relaxed, and Leah smiled. "And we're very grateful for your friendship. How about I get us all some ice cream, including one to replace what fell on the ground?"

Dylan untangled himself from Shane's arms and looked at her. "It was an accident, and Mister Shane told me that he wasn't mad. He even gave me a hug, like you do."

Some of the heaviness in her heart peeled away. She often wondered how much her son blamed her for everything that had happened and whether or not he held anything against her. But it was clear that he saw her as a loving influence, and, selfishly, she was glad Shane was there to witness it. With all the judgment she'd faced in the past, she sometimes wondered if he, too, thought she was a bad mother.

"Good. See? You don't have to be scared of everything. You're surrounded by people who love you."

She got ice cream for everyone, and sitting on Main Street, eating ice cream, Leah felt almost safe. She had a job, which would give her the skills she needed to run her business. And as soon as Harold returned her calls, she would have her cows. Which meant she could finally begin building the life she'd hoped for. This was the happiest she'd felt in a long time.

As they all chatted, mostly about trivial things, Leah once again felt appreciation for the way Shane included her boys. Even Ryan, a squirrely two-year-old, got in the occasional comment.

As they finished their cones, Shane looked over at her. "I was wondering if we can go to the p-a-r-k," he said.

It was sweet of him to try to ask in a way that the boys wouldn't understand. But as soon as the words were out of his mouth, Dylan said, "I know how to spell *park*."

"Park?" Ryan dropped the rest of his cone into the bowl she'd gotten in case he couldn't handle the cone. "Swing!"

Shane looked apologetic, but Leah smiled at him. "It's all right. You tried. Fortunately, I was planning on going to the park. You're right about it being a nice day, and as my sisters have both been telling me a lot lately that I need to learn to have a little fun now and again."

The look he gave her made her feel all tingly inside. Not in some weird teenage way, but something more. Like he saw her as more.

"They're right," he said. "You do work hard. I've had a lot of hired help on my ranch. None of them have been so willing as you. And I see all the things you've done at Helen's. Plus, with raising your boys, you do need a break sometimes. Give yourself a little credit."

As much as she hated to admit it, her sisters had been right. She hadn't realized how desperately she'd needed a day off. Sitting in the sun, watching Shane play horse with her sons, was a nice break. If she'd been at home, she would have been worrying about completing all the things that needed to be done. It was always something. Helen's house, while solid, had definitely been neglected over the years. All the repairs were minor and things she could do on her own. But her sisters said she'd been working too hard, pushing too much. She'd go to Shane's to work during the day, then come home in the evening and work some more. Leah sighed as she closed her eyes and leaned back against the bench. She was tired.

But just as quickly as she'd taken a moment of rest, Dylan came running up to her. "Mom. Mister Shane wants to know if we can go to his house."

She shaded her eyes and looked up at Shane. "Don't we spend enough time at your house? I was thinking you would want to be rid of us for a while."

He smiled at her and joined her on the bench. "Go play with your brother," Shane said to Dylan. "I'm counting on you to look after him while I talk to your mom for a few minutes."

Dylan ran off without complaint. Usually, he took

offense at having to watch his brother, and she was pleased to see the change in him.

Shane turned to her. "I know I should've asked you before I mentioned coming to my house to Dylan. It slipped out. But watching them play, I remembered that I have a swing set in my garage that we could put up. It's nothing as fancy as the park, but I thought it would be something fun for them for while we're working on the barn."

She didn't know what to say. She'd never had an employer take so much interest in her or her children. Sometimes she'd admit that the looks Shane gave her were... She shook her head. It wouldn't do for her to dwell on such thoughts. Dating was the last thing she needed to think about, and Shane had never been inappropriate toward her. All of this was in her head. Where it belonged.

"The spot I'm thinking of putting it, you can see the play area from the barn. But you can be the judge," Shane said, looking at her like he was trying to convince her.

"That's really nice of you. I'm sure the boys would love it."

He glanced over at the boys, then looked at her. "There's also another thing I wanted to ask you. I've noticed that Dylan's behavior has improved over the past few days. With your permission, I'd like to reward him with a ride on my horse."

Dylan had been begging for the opportunity. She liked that Shane was including her on the decision. And asking her privately. It was like he understood her need to control the boys' expectations, to make sure that they were all in a good place. He seemed to be thoughtful in how he approached her. He showed her a level of respect that she'd forgotten could exist between a man and a woman.

Even though she knew his involvement in their lives was because of a promise he made to Helen, he didn't treat her like an obligation. He treated her like a human being he respected.

"That would be great. Dylan asks me every day. I know that it's important to you to maintain control over your animals. So, thank you for this. I know it will mean the world to him."

They gathered up the boys and drove to Shane's ranch. The place was becoming more like home to her, more familiar. There was a sense of pride in driving past the fence she'd repaired. Especially because she'd gone home and done the same to her fences.

Based on the work she'd done at Shane's, she knew she still had a lot of work to do on her ranch to be ready for the cattle. She'd tried explaining that to her sisters, but they hadn't listened. It was a conversation she would have to revisit. But for now, she'd enjoy being at Shane's ranch just for fun.

When they got to the garage, Shane led her to the back, where there was a very nice playset, still in the box, never opened.

"Wow, Mister Shane. That's like the one we had at our old house," Dylan said. "Why do you have a kid swing set?"

Shane cleared his throat, then said, "I used to know a little girl who would've loved it. I saw it on sale, so I bought it, but she never got the chance to use it."

There was a sadness in his voice as he spoke, and Leah wanted to ask what put it there. But she wasn't sure she was ready to hear personal things about Shane's life. She'd already shared way too much about her own than was appropriate. It would be too easy to rely on him, to care about him and to let these weird feelings she was trying to hold back take over. She'd let herself do that once. And while she didn't regret the fact that the two loves of her life had been the result of that union, she wasn't sure she had the strength to do it again. Loving someone during the "for better" was easy, but the "for worse" had nearly killed her.

The swing set was easy enough to build, and it didn't take much time at all. Even with the boys involved, they made quick work of the activity. When they were finished, as promised, Shane took the boys out to the barn.

Ryan was starting to get cranky, and once again she knew that they'd come upon the dreaded naptime.

"You know," Shane said, "I think we should all take a little rest. I've been working hard, and I'm sleepy." He gave an exaggerated yawn.

Leah looked down at the little boy in her arms, who was alternating between struggling to stay awake and trying to remain interested in the activities around him. It was well past naptime, but keeping the boys occupied had staved off some of Ryan's crankiness. Dylan looked like he wanted to argue. Shane, however, held out his hand.

"Come take a rest with me, but then, I promise we'll ride the horse."

Dylan looked at him suspiciously. "Grown-ups don't take naps."

Shane shrugged. "Who said anything about a nap? I just said rest. We'll all go in to the house and close our eyes for thirty minutes. If one of us falls asleep, we'll wait until they wake up."

She had to give him credit. It was a trick she'd often tried. And it only worked sometimes. Still, thirty minutes of rest often did a lot to improve everyone's disposition.

"That sounds like a great idea," Leah said. "I know your brother sure could use it."

A scowl filled Dylan's face. "We always have to do what's good for my brother. Why does he have to be such a baby?"

This again. He'd been so good, but they had been asking a lot of him. She really tried to balance making the boys have time together and giving Dylan a break from his brother.

Shane kneeled in front of Dylan. "It's a lot of responsibility," he said. "But that's the cowboy way. If you want to be a real cowboy, you have to remember to look out for people like your brother, younger than you, smaller than you or maybe just needing a little bit of caring. You have what it takes. That's why we count on you."

Dylan puffed up his chest slightly and stood a little taller. "I am taking cowboy lessons."

Shane nodded. "And you're doing great. That's why I'm ready to let you ride my horse. You think we could wait a little bit longer so that the rest of us could take a break?"

Dylan nodded enthusiastically. Shane had something Leah didn't when it came to influencing her son. He had the right bribe. And she couldn't help but once again appreciate the tenderness with which he talked to her son.

They walked into the house, past the kitchen, in to the family room. "See that chair?" Shane pointed to a worn leather recliner. "That's the best seat in the house."

Dylan looked up at him. "But where will you take your rest?"

Shane pointed to the couch. "I'll sit over there with your mom and brother. The polite thing to do is always to give the best in the house to your guests. I'm offering it to you."

Dylan looked thoughtful for a moment. Then he turned to her. "Mister Shane says that the cowboy way is to take care of women and children. That's what you and Ryan are. So you and Ryan get the comfy chair. I'll stay on the couch with Mister Shane."

Tears tickled the backs of her eyes. She'd been working with her son on being more unselfish, doing more to care for others and putting others before himself. How could she repay Shane for his amazing cowboy lessons that were helping her son learn to be the kind of person she hoped to raise him to be?

Shane opened the lid of the nearby trunk and pulled out blankets. "Take one. We have plenty."

Leah took the blanket he offered and settled into the chair, tucking it around Ryan in her arms. Almost as soon as she was settled, she could feel Ryan's steady breathing turn to sleep. Dylan climbed onto the couch and settled himself in a spot.

He let out a big yawn. "You take the rest you need, and I'll be right here."

Within a minute, her son was asleep. When Leah stole a glance at Shane, he appeared to be sleeping, as well. It was nice to see everyone resting so peacefully. Leah smiled, then let out a long, contented sigh.

It was nice to have this moment of breathing room. And judging from the soft snore coming from Shane, he'd needed a break, too. Part of her felt guilty for imposing on his time. But he seemed to have genuinely enjoyed their day so far.

She hadn't realized she'd fallen asleep until Shane was gently shaking her. "I hate to wake you, but I want to give the boys a chance to ride before dark. I'd like to keep my word to them, but I wanted to let you sleep."

She stretched, yawned and opened her eyes. "It's all right. How long was I sleep?"

"Nearly two hours."

Two hours? "I'm so sorry. I usually don't sleep like this."

"Obviously you needed it. And it was no trouble. The boys and I had a snack. I cut up some apples and spread them with peanut butter the way Dylan said you often do for them. We went out for a swing. I didn't go too far, in case you woke up. You would have been proud of the boys. They behaved themselves, and Dylan even helped me change Ryan's diaper."

She'd never been able to let her guard down like this. Never been able to trust anyone other than her sisters to take care of her boys for a stolen moment of rest. And she always felt so guilty for imposing on them. They had their own lives, their own things they wanted to accomplish. It wasn't fair of her to continually rely on them to do what she should be doing for her sons.

They went out to the barn, where the horse stood, saddled. "Mister Shane helped me brush him. He even held Ryan, so Ryan could have a turn. And Mister Shane told us about all the tack and how to use it. I'm going to be the best cowboy ever. I'm going to be like Mister Shane."

Her son's enthusiasm made her heart melt. It wasn't often that Dylan was so enthusiastic about participating in an activity with his brother. Especially since he'd been forced to do so all day.

"And now you're going to get to ride." Shane gave her a warm smile before turning his gaze on her sons. "This first time, you'll just sit on the horse and get used to him. And then I'll walk you around. It'll take a few times of us doing this, so I know you're comfortable before I let you ride all by yourself."

Shane looked at her son as he explained the rules and Dylan's eyes were right on Shane. It was good to have him so focused. She hoped it was something they could continue. But, she supposed, that would all depend on Dylan's behavior.

Once Dylan was seated on the horse, Shane put Ryan in the saddle with him. "Remember what I said about holding on tight to your brother. He's counting on you to protect him."

She liked the confident way Shane spoke to her son, like he truly believed in him and that Dylan was capable of doing the right thing. She pulled out her phone and took some pictures of the boys riding with Shane. She couldn't remember a time when Dylan sat so tall and proud.

Ryan grinned. "Hor-sey."

Her youngest son's squeal of joy warmed her heart.

Dylan had never looked happier. Hopefully, this would be the very thing they needed to get his behavior on track.

Once the ride was over, Shane helped the boys off

and then gave them jobs to help put away the horse equipment. Even little Ryan had his jobs. Shane would give him brushes and ask him to bring one to his brother or put it away. Small tasks, but it was enough to make both boys understand that they were required to help out. She almost hated to go, but she still needed to get dinner ready, and, somehow, she'd found herself talked into having to bring cookies to church tomorrow for the cookie-and-coffee social they always had afterward.

When she and the boys arrived home, Erin was waiting. "Open your wallet. I want to see that you spent all that money I gave you."

Her sister was such a stickler. Leah let out a long sigh as she looked. "I only spent ten. I took the boys and Shane out for ice cream, then Shane invited us back to his place, where we spent the afternoon."

"Work? You were supposed to take today off."

"I did. We built a swing set that Shane had, so the boys would have something to play on when they came over, and then we took naps, and then Shane took the boys for a ride."

She held out her phone to show her sister the pictures.

Erin scrolled through her screen. "These are so great. Look how happy they are."

Nicole entered the room and Dylan ran to her. "Aunt Nicole! Mister Shane let us ride his horse. He said I'm well on my way to being a real cowboy. If I learn all my lessons, one day I can ride the horse all by myself."

Nicole gave him a big hug. "That's wonderful. You must have been a really good boy to be allowed to do that."

Dylan nodded enthusiastically. "I was. We even let my mom take a nap for two whole hours."

Her sisters stared at her. "Two hours?" Nicole asked. "That's not like you. Are you coming down with something?"

Even Erin stared at her funny.

Leah shook her head. "No. I guess I was really tired. You guys were right about me needing a day off. I'm grateful that Shane was willing and able to take care of the boys so that I could do so. I didn't mean to. It just sort of happened."

Her sisters exchanged knowing glances. Hopefully, their I-told-you-so lecture wouldn't be too long. But her sisters didn't say anything. Instead, they gathered with the boys, who were chatting away about their day with Mister Shane, leaving Leah to go into the kitchen and start dinner. But then Erin joined her soon after.

"So, it was a good day with Mister Shane, was it?"

Leah let out a long sigh. "Yes, but don't be getting any ideas about it."

"I have no ideas that weren't already put there by you. You don't trust anyone with the boys, and I sure can't see you trusting a man. Those boys of yours are already in love with him."

Her sister's words were like a bucket of cold water dumped on her. "Do you think I'm letting him get too close to them?"

Erin groaned. "You're so dense sometimes. I'm not saying that all. I just think it's remarkable that your sons trust him, with everything they've been through. Ryan, not so much, but Dylan? He's been terrified of men since before his father died. If the boys think he's something special, then maybe you should give him a chance, too."

She finished pulling the chicken out of the refrigerator and turned to her sister. "What exactly are you saying?"

"I see the way you two look at each other when you think no one's looking. Maybe you should give Shane a chance."

Leah grabbed the seasoning and turned away from her sister. "Chance of what?"

"Let loose a little. He seems like a good guy, and your sons seem to agree. It wouldn't kill you to go out on a date."

Of all the people to give her such a lecture, Erin should have known better.

She turned back to her sister. "Do I really need to remind you of the bad track record we all have with men?"

Erin shrugged. "So three relationships ended badly. There are millions of other men out there."

"You forgot about our father. He should be enough to put anyone off men forever. Look at poor Helen. She certainly didn't remarry after him."

Erin groaned. "Because there are four bad men out there, we should completely give up on the idea that maybe not all men are horrible?"

"So, if your ex-husband came back and said, hey Erin, let's go out on a date, you would do it?"

"Number one, we aren't talking about me dating again, and two, no one's talking about getting together with an ex. But you know what? Lance isn't a horrible person. I don't regret the time I spent with him. We were both hurting too much to make it work. I would like to think that, someday, there's a chance I'll find love again. I'm sorry if you think that's foolish. But I think it's foolish for you to have a great person looking out for you, who's good with your boys, who obviously likes you, and you act like it's going to ruin your life."

She hadn't thought of it that way, but she also thought that her sister was being a little too hard on her. Erin's ex hadn't been awful the way Leah's had. Maybe her sister couldn't understand her fear of giving away her heart again.

"Please give him a chance. Don't push him away the way you do everyone else. The boys are learning from your example. Don't make them so wary of love because you're afraid to risk your heart."

Such an easy thing for her to say. But, fortunately, that wasn't a bridge Leah needed to cross. "It's not like he's even asked me out. Maybe he really is just being nice."

Erin snorted. "He's not that nice to me and Nicole. Not that he's rude. But you certainly are the object of his special attention. So maybe if you weren't so closed off to him and you gave him an opening, he would. And if he does, and you say no, I'm gonna…"

Her face screwed up like the boys' did when they were angry with each other. "You're going to do what? Punch me in the nose?"

Erin stared at her. "If that's what it takes to knock some sense into you."

Chapter Eight

Shane hadn't been this nervous about going to church in a long time. After having such a great time with Leah yesterday, what would today hold?

He liked her. Really liked her. But as soon as she heard about him buying the cows, she was bound to be furious. It wasn't that he was trying to make her angry. Nor was he trying to start trouble. But it was for the best.

Could he convince her of that? He hoped, as they spent more time together, she learned to trust him and understand that he was only looking out for her and her family. He thought yesterday had been a good example of that. But it was often hard to tell what Leah was thinking, and he never could figure out what set her off.

As soon as the boys saw him, they broke free from Leah and ran to him.

"Mister Shane!" Dylan wrapped his arms around him. Then Ryan followed. If Leah understood how much all of this meant to him, maybe she would understand that he would never in a million years do anything to hurt her or the boys. Maybe some extra prayers were exactly what he needed. And maybe God would help him find a way to make everything work.

"My mom made the cookies today, so you need to be extra good in church, and afterward you can have some." Dylan's enthusiasm made him smile.

All the hard work Leah had been doing to improve her son's behavior and ease the pain from the past seemed to be paying off. It made him feel good being part of it.

Leah approached, her smile guarded. Shane always had a sinking feeling in his stomach when he got that smile. Even though she'd never done so, he longed for the day when she would run up to him the way her boys did, throwing her arms around him with abandon and telling him how happy she was to see him.

"Good morning, Shane," she said. Something flickered in her eyes, but he couldn't tell what it meant. He supposed he had to find some solace in the fact that she no longer looked at him like she'd rather be anywhere but in his company. Maybe he was kidding himself, thinking he and Leah could ever be anything more than friends. Maybe there was a defect in him, wanting women who were clearly emotionally unavailable.

They went into the church, and Leah checked the boys into Sunday school, as she had in the past. But this time Shane waited for her to finish, then turned to her.

"Want to sit together today?"

They always sat separately, but maybe this time they could sit together and get to know each other better, and maybe…

He shook his head. He was as bad as a teenager in youth group. She was here to learn about God, not have him scamming on her. Not that it was a scam. He genuinely cared for her and wanted to know more about her. But as he thought about all her troubles, he knew that the relationship she needed more than anything was one with the Lord.

Leah surprised him by smiling at him. "I'd like that. I've been thinking a lot about what you said, about learning to love one another in church. My sisters have been on me about how I close myself off. Erin and Nicole seem to really love it here, and Erin…"

Leah looked away in the other direction, where her sisters were in conversation with Janie Roberts and a few of the other women. Leah turned back to him. "Erin gave me a stern talking to yesterday, and I don't know that I fully deserved it, but I do think that I should be doing more to give others a chance. So much of Dylan's lashing out is because he expects people to hurt him. We try to teach him otherwise, but…"

A frown marred her forehead. He recognized that look from the times they'd been working and she'd been deep in thought.

Usually, it was like pulling teeth to get her to open up to him like this, but today, her admission came freely. Maybe they'd turned a corner yesterday and were on their way to a better relationship.

Leah looked up at him, some of the wariness gone from her eyes. "She didn't say so, but I've realized that I'm the same way. Because of how badly I've been hurt in the past, I worry that everyone is going to hurt me, even though it's probably not true. I guess, like Dylan, I'm still learning the boundaries of how to balance staying safe and letting others in. Thank you for trying so hard to help me. I know I don't make it easy."

Those words were almost better than the hug he'd hoped to receive from her someday. He couldn't imagine how difficult it had been for her to say that to him, and, in a way, her words shamed him. He was carrying his own baggage, but he hadn't yet trusted her with it. The strains of the opening hymn sounded, and Shane led her into the sanctuary. Hopefully, after church he would have a chance to talk to her about the things in his heart. Just the two of them.

Even though he'd heard sermons on First Corinthians hundreds of times, and he could recite the verses about love being patient and kind from memory, as he stole a glance at Leah, they took on new meaning. He'd thought he'd done all of those things with Gina, and maybe he had, but Gina had never done the same for him. Did Leah know that this was what love was? Was she willing to share that kind of love with him?

Yes, his feelings for her were about the fact that he found her attractive and he liked her personality. But he also knew that there was so much more to her. Would she give him the chance to let him see it?

A woman approached Leah and whispered something in her ear. Leah's face turned white. Funny how Shane didn't even need to hear what had been said to know what it was about. What had Dylan done this time?

When Leah got up, Shane followed. She didn't say anything until they were out in the main hallway, but then she turned to him. "You don't have to come," she said. "I can handle it."

So they were back to this. But just because Leah

pushed him away didn't mean he had to let her. "I know, but I still want to be here for you, if that's okay."

Leah nodded slowly. "Thank you. It's not necessary, but I appreciate the gesture."

He followed her to the Sunday-school classroom, then out the door to the playground. Dylan was standing in the corner, facing out, rocks in his hands. Tears were running down his face, and he once again saw the wounded boy he'd first met.

Leah walked over to him, slowly, calmly. "What's going on?"

Dylan made a motion like he was going to throw the rock, but he didn't. "That boy was teasing me for not having a dad," he said, the grief obvious in his voice.

"His words must have really hurt you," Leah said gently.

"It's not fair. How come everyone else gets to have a dad? A good dad?"

The sadness in his voice made Shane feel weak at the knees. He took a step toward the little boy. "I don't have a dad, either," he said.

Leah looked at him. "Really? You've never talked about your family, but I assumed…"

Shane took another step forward. One day, there would be time for him to explain his past to Leah. But right now, a little boy needed him. "My dad ran off when I was about your age. I'm told he's still alive somewhere, but I've never heard from him. My mom married another guy. And he was mean. My older brothers tried to protect me, but they would just get hurt, too, so they moved away. As soon as I was old enough to leave home, I did."

He hadn't thought about this part of his past in a long time. It had been so long ago that he'd been able to move on, accepting that he had no family to speak of. But maybe speaking of it would help a certain little boy.

Dylan sniffled. "Did people make fun of you, too?"

Shane nodded. "Every day. Sometimes the kids at school would beat me up. And that's why I decided to become a cowboy, so I could protect others like me."

Sniffling again, Dylan looked up at him. "That's why you're teaching me how to be a cowboy, isn't it?"

Shane nodded. Until now, it hadn't occurred to him how much he had in common with this little boy. Dylan had that same hunger for a male influence in his life that he had had. In Shane's case, he'd been fortunate enough to meet Helen and Norm, who'd given him a job and shown him a new way of life.

He hadn't been a little boy when he met them, but he'd also needed the same love and tenderness.

"I know what that boy said hurt you," Shane said. "I'd be hurt, too. But cowboys don't deal with their hurt by picking up a rock and trying to hurt people back. It's tempting, because you want that person to hurt the same way you did. But then they only want to hurt someone again. If we keep hurting each other, then all anybody does is hurt."

He held his hand out to Dylan. "So, how about we go talk to that boy, and we figure out a way to be friends?"

Dylan threw down the rocks and ran to him, wrapping his arms around him. "Why can't you be my dad?"

"Because being someone's dad takes a lot of work

between the grown-ups. I have to fall in love with your mom, and she has to fall in love with me. And then, we have to get married. That doesn't happen overnight. But I can sure be your friend."

Dylan hugged him tight, then looked up at him. "My mom likes pancakes a lot. If you bring her pancakes every day, maybe she'll fall in love with you, and then you can be my dad."

Was it wrong to wish the same? Shane gave him another squeeze. "It takes a lot more than pancakes to make someone fall in love," he said. "But your mom is a good woman, and I'm sure that someday someone good will fall in love with her."

"What about you?"

He could feel Leah's eyes on him. The trouble was, he still didn't know the right answer to that question. Not in a way that wouldn't get anyone's hopes up or make anyone feel bad.

"Tell you what. You leave the falling in love to the grown-ups. Focus on being a good cowboy. And maybe one day, we can talk about all that other stuff."

Dylan turned to his mom. "I'm sorry for getting in trouble."

Then he turned back to Shane. "I'm sorry for not being a good cowboy."

Shane gave him a smile. "We all make mistakes. As long as we learn from them, that's the important thing. What did you learn from making a mistake?"

Dylan let out a long sigh. "That even if someone says mean things to me, I shouldn't be mean back."

They entered the classroom together and Dylan walked over to his teacher, Jenny. "I'm sorry," he said.

She held her arms out to him. "And I'm sorry, too. I

forgot that some boys don't have fathers to make cards for on Father's Day."

Dylan looked over at Shane, then back at her. "Could I make a card for a friend instead?"

The parents were already arriving to pick up the children to go home, but Jenny nodded. "Of course. I should have made that offer to begin with."

Paul Bartlett walked in the room with his little boy. "What's this about a new boy picking a fight with my son?"

Shane turned and looked at him. "Apparently, your son teased him for not having a dad."

Paul snorted and shook his head. "You and your project women. Maybe it's time you picked someone other than a single mom. Stupid women, leeching off our society. Maybe they should start by getting married first, then having babies."

No wonder Dylan had gotten into a fight with his kid.

Leah straightened, then turned to look at Paul. "Actually, I'm a widow. I am a single mom but not by choice. I would imagine that a lot of the single moms that you're so down on are in a similar position. We're all doing the best we can, and it would do you a world of good to have a little compassion. And teach your son to do the same."

The strength in her voice made him want to applaud, especially because Paul did look ashamed of himself.

"I'm sorry. I meant no harm. But in these times, you can see where it would be easy to assume otherwise."

Leah shook her head. "No, I can't. Based on what I heard in the sermon today, you should be reaching out to the single moms and helping them. You should be doing that for everyone, not just the people you think are worthy. Nowhere in First Corinthians does it say to love only the people who are worthy of love."

He nodded slowly, then looked down at Dylan. "I'm sorry about your dad." He nudged his son. "Aren't we?"

The other boy nodded. "Yeah. That must be terrible to have your dad die. Who do you play catch with?"

Dylan looked up at Leah. "My mom."

Shane wanted to hug the little boy and tell him that he didn't need a dad. He had the most amazing mom in the world. He wished he'd had a mom like Leah.

Paul looked over at Leah. "I'm real sorry to hear about your husband. If there is anything you need, you give us a call. I'm sure it's hard, not having any menfolk around."

Leah looked over at Shane. "Thank you. Shane has been wonderful with helping out, but if I do need anything, I'll let you know."

He could tell by the tone in her voice that Paul was the last person she'd ever call on if she needed anything. But he seemed mollified by her answer and nodded as he escorted his son out of the room.

Jenny handed Dylan a piece of paper and a stack of stickers. "I had to put the markers and things away, so you might have to use some stuff from home. But I thought I would give you a few things you can use to make your card."

Dylan nodded at her. "Thank you." His polite answer made Shane smile. The little boy was going to be all right.

When they walked out of the classroom, all the

cookies were gone. Dylan's fists balled up. "I really wanted you to have one of my mom's cookies, Mister Shane."

The little boy's eyes were still red from crying, and the way Leah tensed, he knew that the worst wasn't over.

"I know you did, buddy, but looks like everyone else enjoyed them. Maybe sometime we could make them together. That way your mom doesn't have to do all the work herself."

Leah smiled at him. "That sounds like a great idea. We all like to bake cookies. I saved some back at the house for dessert tonight. Maybe you'd like to come over for dinner?"

Before he could answer, Susan, one of the nursery workers, came up to them, carrying Ryan. "I know you were busy with your other son, but we're trying to get the nursery closed down. Is it okay if I leave him with you now?"

Leah held her arms out for her son. "Of course. I am so sorry. I can't believe I forgot to come get him."

Susan smiled. "It's all right. One of the other nursery workers let us know what was going on. I'm sorry about my husband. Paul can be pretty intense in expressing his opinion. I hope you know that you are very welcome here, and when things settle down, I'd really love to get our boys together for a play date. Joshua can be a handful, as can my husband. But they really aren't so bad when you get to know them."

Leah nodded. "I'd like that. I'm really hoping that once school starts, Dylan knows a few people so he doesn't feel so overwhelmed. And I really appreciate you being willing to give my son another chance.

I admit, he's got some behavioral issues, but we are working on them."

Susan smiled at her. "All kids have behavioral issues. I think the best way to deal with them is to love and accept the child, so the child doesn't feel like they have to act out all the time. I'm sorry that your son has experienced hurtful responses to his behavior. And like I said, I can't apologize enough for what my husband and son said. I'm really trying to raise him better than that."

As the two women chatted, Shane said a silent prayer of thanks that the situation, which seemed to be headed in a bad direction, had turned out so positively for Leah. She'd even managed to develop a friendship as a result. Or at least the beginnings of one.

Though Leah had the love and friendship of her sisters, it was good for her to meet another woman who could love and accept her as a friend at church. He only hoped that Susan followed through with her promise of a play date and that things would continue to blossom between the two women.

He could only hope she didn't get let down again.

But knowing more about Leah's past with her late husband, he did have to give her credit. It took a lot of strength to choose to stay with someone under those circumstances. He didn't know what he would've done in her shoes. Maybe that's why God taught them not to judge. Because unless you were in that situation, you couldn't possibly know the best way to handle it.

He was glad Leah had asked him to dinner. He wanted to steal away with her for a few minutes, so he could tell her how brave she was. So he could tell her about Gina, his past, and even his special connection to Leah's son. It would take more than a few minutes, but he hoped this conversation would lead to many more over the course of their lives.

It was weird to think that she might have made a new friend at church over her son fighting with another boy. But Susan had seemed very understanding, and Leah looked forward to getting to know her better in and out of church. Maybe it was time to start giving others a chance.

As if on cue, Shane arrived to dinner with a bouquet of flowers, an unexpected treat. She thought about what Erin had said to her. Maybe Shane did like her, but she had been so intent on pushing him away that he didn't feel safe expressing it. She wasn't even sure how she felt about liking him, but she hadn't done much in the way of dealing with that, either.

"Thank you, these are beautiful." She wanted to pat herself on the back for not saying something like, "You shouldn't have." It had to mean something that she was trying.

"You're very welcome. You deserve to be spoiled every now and again," he said.

Erin joined them. "Exactly what I've been telling her. Sometimes she acts like the weight of the world is upon her shoulders, but it's okay for her to relax and indulge a little."

She turned and glared at her sister. "And I've been doing a very nice job of taking your advice this weekend, so back off."

To her credit, Erin did take a step back. Literally.

Shane chuckled. "So, this is sisterly love? I'm glad I had three brothers."

"I didn't know you had family," Erin said. "You'll have to tell us about them."

"Not much to tell. I left home when I was seventeen, and I haven't been back since. We never kept in touch. Helen and her brother took me in and treated me like their own. I hope it doesn't sound too terrible, but they've been more my family than anyone else."

All this time, she hadn't thought much about where Shane had come from. What his story was. But after what happened earlier at church, she was curious.

Dinner went well, and Leah was happy that everyone behaved, including Erin. Every once in a while, she and Nicole would giggle at some secret joke they shared, but to their credit, neither said anything.

After dinner, Leah stood to clear the table, but Erin stopped her. "No, you don't. It's our turn. The boys will help us. Take Shane to the porch and have a cup of coffee while we clean everything up."

Could her sister be any more obvious? Though she'd asked Erin to back off, in this instance she was glad for the interference. She did have questions for Shane. Things that seemed to have been unspoken between them a lot the past couple of days, but, because the boys were around, they hadn't been able to discuss.

"Thanks. That sounds great."

She wanted to stick her tongue out at her sister, who had probably been expecting an argument, but she'd try to be a good example for her boys.

They sat on the swing, one of Leah's many projects. It had been old and worn, with peeling paint, but she'd sanded and repainted it. She'd had great hopes of spending quiet evenings out here, looking out over the ranch. But quiet evenings with her boys were few and far between.

Leah looked over at Shane. "I suppose I should apologize for that blatant attempt at matchmaking."

He shook his head. "Don't. I've been wanting to get you alone for a while now. It seems like we both have things on our mind we would like to talk about, but it's challenging to do with the boys around."

At least they were on the same page. "But the matchmaking…"

Shane shook his head. "Don't worry about it. Like I told Dylan today, falling in love is something that happens between the two people who fall in love, and no one else. Even though your sisters are pushing us together, you have to make the right decisions for you, not them, not even the boys. Obviously, you don't want to choose someone who'd be bad for them, but that isn't something you'd do. You can want them to have a dad all you want, but don't let that guide your decision about having a relationship. I can always be their friend."

She nodded slowly, remembering one of the jabs from the guy at church. "Does this have anything to do with Paul's comment about you being into single moms?"

Shane looked away for a moment, then turned his attention back to her. "It's not as bad as all that. I dated a single mom a while back. I thought I was in love with her, but she was just looking for a father for her daughter. Natalie was a good kid, and I spent a lot of time with her. I took care of her like my own."

Then he let out a long sigh. "But Gina met someone else, someone more exciting, and she took off with him. Obviously, Natalie went with her. Broke my heart. But

I've realized that the mistake I made was in trying to be Natalie's father, when I wasn't. Gina let me, because it was easy for her. But the thing about it is, because I wasn't Natalie's dad, when Gina left, I had no right to Natalie. And that's not something I'm willing to do again. I'll always be there for your boys, as a friend. But if something happens between you and me, I want it to be about the two of us. Like I said, I want you to fall in love with me because you love me, not because your children need a father."

His words comforted her, not just because he was making the conversation about them, but because he was letting her see deep inside him. She wanted a man who, like her, only wanted someone to love. She'd thought that with her family to raise and all her responsibilities, it was too much to ask. But now, as she sat on the swing with Shane, she couldn't help wondering if it were possible.

Not that she'd admit such things to Erin anytime soon.

"That's what I want, too. It's just harder when you have children, because you have a responsibility to protect them. I want to make sure that if I bring a man around them, he is someone I can count on."

Shane nodded slowly. "That's wise. I can tell you all I want that I'm a good guy, but only you know what's best for your children."

His approval shouldn't matter so much to her, and yet, it felt good to know he was on her side. He'd seen her and her kids at their worst and still respected her as a mother. So many people didn't.

Maybe that's why she'd spent so much time being closed off. She'd already faced so much judgment from others. Here in Columbine Springs, however, not everyone judged her harshly. She'd expected to have been run off from church today after the way Dylan had behaved, and yet, everyone acted with understanding. No one in the hallways shook their heads at her in disappointment. They must have known what had happened, but not one person stepped forward to condemn her.

And Shane, despite everything he'd witnessed and everything she'd told him, was still here with her, opening up about his past, wanting to pursue her.

She scooted a little closer to him. "I'm not very good at this," she said. "Jason was my high school sweetheart, and I've never dated anyone else. How do I know that I'm making the right decision for myself and for the boys?"

She definitely needed work on sounding smoother. But at least Shane didn't seem to mind. He took her hand. "You're doing fine. We all have to approach a relationship in our own way. I hope you know that I care about you."

He looked like he wanted to say something else, but then he shook his head and gazed out across the field.

For a few minutes, the only sound was the creak of the swing, the whisper of the breeze and the occasional cricket chirping in the distance.

Then Shane turned to her. "My feelings for you aren't just about keeping a promise to Helen. I like you. A lot. I'm trying to balance doing what I think is right for you and your family with my feelings for you. I know that you have more than just yourself to consider."

His words made her heart twist in a funny way. Romance was supposed to be about love and butterflies, but it seemed infinitely more romantic to be liked. Being liked meant he looked beyond the surface, into her heart, and appreciated what he saw.

"Thank you," she said. "Sometimes I don't know if I'm doing the right thing or not, but when I'm with you, you give me confidence I wasn't sure I had."

The look he gave her reminded her a lot of Helen. Growing up, Helen had been one of the few people in her life to make her believe in herself. Obviously, she'd taught Shane to do the same.

"I know sometimes you think you can't tell the right or wrong way to go. But today's lesson in First Corinthians is a good guide. Ask yourself if it leads you closer or further from love. And to define love, you've got to use what the Bible says."

She hadn't thought of it that way, but as she pondered Shane's words, they made a lot of sense. As she mentally went through the list of words defining love, like patience and kindness, she could see where trusting Shane was the right thing to do.

"We spend so many years of our lives thinking love is about butterflies, but you're right. Love is so much more."

His gentle smile warmed her as he squeezed her hand tighter. "I'm not going to lie and say there aren't butterflies. But at least now you understand when I tell you that I want more than that. We both deserve that kind of love."

Tears sprang to her eyes. Until now, the idea of love and romance in her life was a secret wish. One she hadn't much allowed herself to indulge in. Like the secret stash of chocolate Erin had hidden away.

Shane used his free hand to brush at her tears. "What are those for?"

"Because you make me think that so much of what I've been denying myself might be possible."

It wasn't like her to be so honest about her feelings. But she also hadn't felt safe enough to do so in a long time.

He ran his hand straight down her cheek, then cupped her chin. Then he tilted her chin up to him. "You deserve to have your dreams come true."

When he bent and kissed her, it was a gentle, fleeting touch that jolted her to the very core. His kiss held the warmth of the promise of the future. One with a man who wanted to be her partner, who believed in her and had shown her time and again that she could count on him.

As she kissed him back, he shifted his position, so he could put his arms around her, pulling her close to him and holding her tight.

Slowly, he broke the kiss, then gave her a squeeze before kissing her on top of her head.

"I might have gotten carried away," he said. "I'm pretty sure that was the best kiss of my life, but I hope you know that's not what this is about."

"I wouldn't have let you kiss me if I thought otherwise." She smiled as she closed her eyes briefly, reliving the way he'd touched her. How long had it been since she'd been comfortable in a man's arms?

She hadn't gotten far in her memory when a voice rang out, "Does this mean you're going to get married?"

Her eyes flew open as she saw Dylan standing in the doorway with Erin.

"I…"

Shane scooted away. "No," he said. "I told you, marriage is something that happens between grown-ups. And you have to give them space to make up their minds."

Erin chuckled. "Seems to me you were doing quite a bit of making out—I mean, up."

Leah glared at her sister. She wasn't making things any better.

"It was just a kiss."

Erin snorted. "That was some kiss."

Looking down at her son, Leah said, "That wasn't meant for you to see. Shane is right. We still have a lot of grown-up things to work out between us, but I promise, you will be the first to know if anything serious happens between me and Shane."

Erin looked like she was going to say something, but Leah glared at her again. "Why don't you take Dylan back inside and we'll join you in a few minutes?"

She seemed to have gotten the message, because she nodded slowly as she guided Dylan back into the house.

Leah turned her attention back to Shane. "That's not what I wanted to happen."

"I'm sorry. I wasn't thinking. I should have known better than to have kissed you here, where the boys could see."

The disappointment in his voice made her feel guilty. She hadn't meant to hurt him. "It's not that I'm ashamed of you or that I didn't enjoy the kiss. I need time to figure out our relationship before the boys get invested in the idea of us being together."

Who was she kidding? Dylan was already one hundred percent invested in the notion of having Shane be his dad. But everything Shane had said was correct. Their relationship couldn't be about the boys. It had to be about Leah and Shane deciding to make a relationship work for their own sakes and then committing their relationship to her sons.

"I understand," Shane said. "I completely agree. We'll keep things on a friendship-slash-working level for now, and we'll figure the other stuff out as we can."

The regret in his voice gave her hope. He wanted things to work just as much as she did, but it was just as important to him to keep her boys safe.

But who was going to keep her safe? She'd thought she was protecting her heart, but as the final rays of sun fell over the mountains in the distance, she was afraid she'd already gone and fallen in love.

Chapter Nine

Even though he'd checked his reflection in the shop windows as he passed to make sure his feet were on the ground, Shane felt like he was flying higher than the clouds as he went to meet Leah at the café. They'd spent the entire week working together with the boys, doing their best to keep any romance at bay. But today, Erin had the day off and she was keeping the kids so they could have some grown-up time.

Leah might resent her sister's matchmaking, but having an ally gave Shane the confidence that they could make things work.

The giddy feeling, however, disappeared the moment he stepped into the café.

Harold was sitting at a table by the entrance. Leah stood nearby, talking to him.

"What do you mean, you sold the cattle to someone else? I thought we had a deal."

To most listeners, the screech in her voice would have been imperceptible. But Shane knew it well. It was the sound of Leah desperately trying to hang on when everything around her was falling apart. It usually only happened during one of Dylan's fits.

But this one was all Shane's fault.

"Who did you sell to?"

Harold gestured at him. "Sounds like you need to have a talk with Shane. He approached me."

Though he imagined she'd probably turned very quickly to face him, everything appeared to happen in slow motion. Enough that he could hear the blood rushing through his veins and couldn't manage to move his mouth to form a single coherent word.

"Why didn't you tell me?"

He should've been better prepared for this moment. He'd known it was coming, but he hadn't been able to face it. Now he had no choice. But he still had no words.

"I tried, but I didn't know how."

He deserved all the fire in her glare. It would have been enough to melt the polar ice caps.

"It's really quite simple," she said. "Leah, I bought the cows you wanted."

She took a step toward him, and he could see spots of rage covering every inch of her face. "Seven words. You're a grown man. You can't say seven words?"

Not those words.

"I was trying to find a way to explain. It's not as simple as it sounds."

Her eyes flashed, and he could practically see the steam rising from her head. "Try me."

Everyone in the café was staring at them. The last thing he wanted was a public spectacle, especially because the romance was bound to come up in this argument.

"How about we go somewhere private, and we'll discuss it?"

Unfortunately, she seemed to take offense at his suggestion. "Why? So you have time to come up with a new story? Just give it to me straight."

He took a deep breath, saying a quick prayer that God would help him find the right words.

"Even though I had explained the risks about taking on the cattle, you were unwilling to listen to reason. If I couldn't convince you, how could I convince your sisters? It seemed easier for everyone if I took on the herd."

Why had he thought she'd understand? He hadn't expected it to make her so much angrier.

"You told me you didn't want to take on the project. You said it was too much for you. Why did you lie to me?"

She had a point. "I was telling the truth. They are too much for me. A friend is letting me keep them on his land, and I'm getting a break on the vet bills. They know the severity of what's happening with these cows, and, like me, they want to minimize the risk to the community. But still, it's been hard."

He'd been planning to ask around after breakfast to see if anyone could hire him for some odd jobs or something. He hadn't been exaggerating when he'd said taking on the cattle was going to be expensive. Buying them, plus paying Leah, plus the added expense of their care had taken a toll on his finances.

She'd probably say he deserved it.

And maybe he did.

"So, you brought others in on your scheme?" she asked, her voice growing eerily quiet. "You really thought I was so stupid and illogical you had to step in and make a decision for me by taking it away?"

Maybe a relationship wouldn't have worked out between them. Not when she automatically jumped to conclusions and believed the worst about him.

"I don't think you're stupid. You're one of the smartest people I know. But when it comes to ranching, you are too inexperienced to understand the dangers of the situation."

Her glare intensified.

How could he get her to believe his intentions were good? That his heart was in the right place?

"The herd was in a worse state than you were led to believe. They were half-starved, and many had not received the required vaccinations. Since I took them on over a week ago, I've already lost three head. The vet is testing for cause of death to make sure it wasn't a communicable disease. These are not starter cows."

Tears ran down her face, and he wanted to comfort her, but he knew it would only anger her more.

"Why couldn't you have let me make that decision for myself? You could have offered to bring me and my sisters to see the cattle and explain to us what this meant. But you rode in on that big white horse of yours and took over."

That wasn't what he'd intended. But everyone knew where the road paved with good intentions led.

"I'm sorry. I did the best I could in the moment. When I took on the cows, you still didn't trust me, and it seemed like we had a long way to go."

The look she gave him was a dagger to his heart. "I should have never let my guard down around you. This proves what I feared all along. I can't trust you.

I should have known better than to trust anyone. I don't know what your agenda is, but I'm done letting it play out here."

"I'm sorry," he said. "Please give me the chance to make it up to you."

Tears continued to stream down her face as she shook her head. "People ask me how I stayed with a drug addict for so long. It's because of promises like that. 'I promise I'll do better. I promise I'll make it up to you.' Guess what? I'm done believing those promises."

So that's where she wanted to take it. Comparing him to a drug addict. He supposed he deserved some condemnation, but this felt a little extreme. He'd only hurt her once. And he was willing to make it up to her.

"This isn't it the same, and you know it. I was going to tell you eventually. I just needed more time."

"More time for what? To cook up a good story? Interesting that you're keeping these cows on somebody else's land, and yet all the times I've helped you, worked on your land, taking care of your animals, you've never mentioned having this herd someplace else. If the whole point of working with you is for me to learn about ranching, why wouldn't you have brought me there? You could have given me the chance to work with sick cows so I would know what to do. I know all about smokescreens. And this is the biggest one I've ever seen."

Her vision was too clouded by her pain from her past to see what he was trying to tell her. But for the sake of two little boys who would be devastated if they parted as enemies, he had to try.

"I would have loved to get your help with the other

cows. By the time you get to my ranch in the mornings, I've already been at it for two hours, trying to keep up. But I can't risk bringing your children around sick cattle. I'm sorry if it seemed deceptive. I was truly doing what I thought was in everyone's best interest."

He shouldn't have opened his mouth.

Leah shook her head at him. "And here I thought you were letting me make decisions about my children, not taking over for me. That didn't work out so well for you before, now did it? You should have told me. Explained the risks. And given me credit as their mother to make that decision."

Clearly, they weren't going anywhere with this conversation. The café was silent, everyone completely fixated on what was happening between them. And no matter what he said, things were only getting worse.

He took off his hat and held it in his hands as he looked at her. "I don't know how I can express to you how truly sorry I am for going behind your back and buying the cows out from under you. I thought I was doing the right thing. I know now that I made a lot of missteps along the way. I hope someday you can find it in your heart to forgive me for what I've done."

Leah shook her head. "That might be what the church says I have to do, and maybe someday I'll get there. But right now, I hope you'll understand when I say that you are no longer welcome on my ranch."

Then she hesitated. "That is, except to check on your cattle under the terms of your lease. But you'd best talk to your friend about using his land for when your lease expires. Please do not attempt to further our acquaintance, nor communicate with my children. You've proven that you can't be trusted."

She stepped forward, like she was headed for the door, but then she stopped. "I hope it goes without saying that I no longer consider myself your employee. I won't work with someone who is so dishonest. I may not have much, and I might be desperate, but I'm not so desperate as to compromise my integrity."

She continued out the café, and he let her go. It was best to let her cool down and give her time to realize that he wasn't a malicious person. Everything he'd ever done had been for the good of her family and the community. Maybe someday she would realize that.

And as the last pieces of his heart shattered like the mug Dylan had destroyed, he had to admit that perhaps this was a sign that their relationship wasn't meant to be.

He'd asked God for a deep, abiding love. Maybe Leah was too broken to give him that. So, maybe he had to accept that she wasn't the right woman for him after all.

Harold stood. "I didn't know my cows were in such bad shape," he said.

"Everyone else in this town did. Except for three desperate women who didn't know any better."

Harold looked embarrassed, but it didn't feel strong enough. Given the condition of the cattle, it seemed almost like an insult.

"You should be brought up on animal cruelty charges. Those women wouldn't have stood a chance. As it is, I'm not sure how I'm going to make it."

Harold left, which should have made it easy to grab a table and breakfast. But Shane found he'd lost his appetite completely. He didn't feel like doing much of anything at all.

He turned to go home, but Fred Novak, who ran the feed store, stopped him. "I'm sorry to hear about your troubles. I know your heart was in the right place, buying those cows. I had a look at them myself a month ago and turned Harold down. I warned him they needed better care, and I'm disappointed to hear that he didn't listen."

At least someone believed him. But it didn't feel as comforting as the man had probably intended.

Still, he meant well. And people needed to be given credit for that. "Thank you. I appreciate it."

"If there's anything I can do to help you, you let me know."

"You wouldn't happen to have any jobs available, would you?"

Fred nodded. "Actually, I do. I should warn you. Leah applied for it, and I had to turn her down, because she wasn't available much due to her childcare issues. But I know you're a good worker, and with my son Colton joining the service, I could use the help."

Leah probably would get upset with him when she found out, but it was a job. Even with getting a break on the vet bills, they were still more than he could afford easily. Not having to pay Leah would lessen some of that burden, especially because taking the time to teach her things slowed him down.

But it hadn't bothered him because he'd enjoyed her company, and he'd thought he was doing the right thing by helping her.

So much for doing the right thing. Women all said they wanted a good guy, but it seemed like being the good guy led to getting his heart broken.

* * *

Leah couldn't honestly say how she got home. She'd obviously driven, but if she had passed a circus with a giant bear dancing in the streets, she wouldn't have noticed. She'd spent the entire drive crying.

Was there anyone in this world who could be honest with her? Who didn't go sneaking around her back, lying?

All right, so Shane hadn't lied. That she would give him. But he had gone behind her back. He had deceived her. In a most painful way.

She'd actually allowed herself to hope that they could have a relationship. But what use was a relationship when there wasn't open communication? When she looked back on her marriage, the biggest problem hadn't been Jason's drug use. No, it had been the fact that there had been so much he'd kept from her. Whether it was how bad the pain was or how stressed out he was or how overwhelmed he felt by the pressures of parenting. He'd told her none of those things. He'd wanted to prove that he was the big, strong man. That he could take care of his family. So many of his decisions, especially the wrong ones, had been because he'd thought he was protecting her.

She barely hit the front porch when Erin came out. "What happened?"

"Shane."

Erin's face fell. "What did he do? I would've never pegged him as the type to hurt a woman."

She wiped the tears away with her sleeve. "He didn't hurt me. At least not physically. But the next time I tell you to back off when it comes to my romantic life, you'd better listen. I took a chance, just like you told me. And now I have to figure out what to tell my boys so they understand they will never be allowed around that lying snake again."

Erin's brow furrowed. "What did he do?"

Wiping her eyes again, Leah took a deep breath. "Remember those cows we were supposed to get?"

Her sister nodded.

"Shane decided we couldn't handle it, but rather than discussing it with us, he took the choice away. He bought those cows out from under us, and then he hid them so we wouldn't find out."

Erin stared at her. "Are you sure? There has to be some mistake. I thought you told me that Shane said he couldn't afford the cows."

She couldn't remember Shane's exact words, but she was certain he'd said something to that effect. "That's what he'd led me to believe. But yes, he did it. He told me so himself."

Wrapping her arms around her, Erin said, "I'm so sorry. He seemed like such a nice guy. Did he give you any indication as to why he would do it?"

She stepped back from her sister's embrace. "Because he was worried that we were getting in over our heads. He didn't trust us to make the right decision."

Erin put her arm around her and led her inside the house. "Why do men always think they know better than we do? I can't believe he didn't even talk to you about it."

The bitterness in her sister's voice reminded Leah that Erin had plenty of experience with men who didn't communicate. Her marriage broke down for a lot of reasons, but in the end, Erin's divorce was really about her ex-husband's unwillingness to communicate with her about anything of importance, including their shared grief over the loss of their daughter.

Maybe it was the whole Mars-Venus thing, that men and women were from different planets and completely incapable of understanding one another. Maybe some people could live like that, but what Leah wanted in a romantic relationship was a full partnership. Communication. Friendship. And most of all, trust.

The part that hurt the most about Shane's decision, besides the fact that she couldn't trust him, was that his actions showed he didn't trust her. He didn't believe that she would make the right decision.

True, she was planning on buying the cows anyway, but she had considered his advice. If the cows were in as bad a shape as Shane claimed, they would have sought further counsel. But Shane wasn't willing to give her that much credit. He wasn't willing to sit down with her and tell her his plan. Instead, he took the choice away from her, like he thought she was a child.

They entered the kitchen, and Nicole was in there, covered in flour.

"I wasn't expecting you back so soon. The boys and I are making homemade slime. The ingredients are all natural and healthy, so is—" She stopped. "What happened?"

The boys were staring at her. She hated the look on Dylan's face. He didn't know yet that she'd had a falling out with his precious Mister Shane, but he had seen her crying way too many times. No child should have to witness their mother's broken heart. And poor Dylan seemed to know it best of all. It wasn't fair.

"It's okay. Mommy's just having a really tough day."

Dylan climbed off his seat and wrapped his arms around her. Then Ryan did the same. Their hands were sticky and covered in whatever concoction Nicole had been teaching them to make, but it felt wonderful. This was where she belonged. The idea of romance had been tempting, but it came at a price too high to ignore.

"Where's Mister Shane?" Dylan asked. "I thought you were going to work with him today."

She let out a long breath, trying to keep it steady. "Unfortunately, I won't be working with Mister Shane anymore. It's not a good job for Mommy after all."

She didn't know how to explain the situation to the boys. Not when it was all about the kind of grown-up stuff they'd already been cautioned about. She could see the disappointment on her son's face, and there was nothing she could do about it.

"But I was going to help Mister Shane with the animals. He told me I could." Dylan's upper lip quivered. "I need to learn how to be a cowboy, so I can help with our ranch."

The ache in Leah's stomach worsened. Her son had thrived under Shane's care, but how could she explain to Dylan that she couldn't trust a man who went behind her back? If he'd go behind her back about this, what else would he go behind her back on? What would happen if they disagreed on something concerning Dylan?

"I think you've done really well on your cowboy lessons," she finally said. "I'm going to need all your help on our ranch. All the things we did on Mister Shane's ranch, we're going to do here."

Nicole passed out damp paper towels. "Let's clean up. Everyone needs to wash their hands. And your mom is right. You're going to be too busy with our animals to help with Mister Shane's." She held out her hand. "Come on. Let's go look at that website with the animals again."

Nicole and the boys scampered into the other room, where the computer was. Erin returned to Leah's side.

"I'm sorry this happened. I was so focused on en-couraging you that it didn't occur to me that things might not work out. I'd forgotten that your heart wasn't the only one to be broken."

Tears filled her eyes again. She hated that it took something so painful to make her sister understand why interfering was such a bad idea. But at least she wouldn't make the same mistake again. Neither of them would. Being alone was a small price to pay for the happiness and security of her children.

Somehow she got through the rest of the morning and lunch. Probably only because she had her sisters to help her. That was the other trouble with being heart-broken. She still had a life to live, children to raise. She didn't have time to mourn or grieve or dwell on her pain. Even though what she really wanted was to have a good cry.

Fortunately, the boys didn't put up a fuss about taking a rest. Though visiting the animal website had taken away Dylan's questions about Mister Shane, they all felt a heaviness at the loss. She would talk to Nicole about the best way to handle it. Once the boys were lying down, she went to make herself a cup of tea, but Erin had already done so.

"Here," she said. "Now that we have a little time, we can talk about what happened."

They went into the family room, and each sister took up her usual spot. It was comfortable, familiar. At least something felt normal after everything that had happened.

She relayed the morning's events to the sisters, once again feeling the pain of Shane's betrayal. Both sisters nodded and murmured at the appropriate places, and it felt good to know they were on her side.

"If it's really that bad, I guess he saved us," Erin said. "But he should have talked to you first. He should have talked to all of us. It wasn't fair for him to put the entire burden of the decision-making on you. It wasn't just your decision, but he treated you like it was. If he had concerns, he should have brought them to us, rather than relying on you to relay the message."

Erin's frustration at the situation gave Leah a little more confidence.

Nicole nodded. "Exactly. He never once spoke to us. I hate how men swoop in and rescue women that don't need rescuing." Then she sighed. "All right, I'll admit that based on what he said about the condition of the cows, maybe we did. But he could have given us the opportunity to make that decision for ourselves."

Her phone buzzed, and she looked down at it. "This is exactly what I mean. Fernando again. I'm sick of him bugging me, trying to make sure I'm all right. I've told him a thousand times that I'm fine, so why can't he accept my answer and move on? That's what any woman wants. But none of the men in our lives have ever understood that."

She was talking about their father, even though she hadn't mentioned the Colonel. But they were all thinking about him, based on the expression on Erin's face, as well. He'd been so controlling, so possessive. He'd dictated every aspect of their lives, and probably would've continued to do so had he not met cute, young wife number-whatever-she-was, who'd decided she was too young to have children so old.

They didn't often speak of the Colonel, mostly because none of them wanted to relive those memories. But, also, for the most part they'd gotten over what life with him had been like. Leah could remember some of the underhanded ways he'd asserted his control, just like Shane.

She didn't deserve her sisters' support, not when she'd let them down so badly.

"I don't know what I'm going to do about a job," she said. "I'm not even sure how I'll get paid for the work I've already done for Shane. I don't want to have to talk to him again to find out, but I know we could use the money."

Erin came and sat down next to her. "Don't worry about the money. Nicole and I both have good jobs, and now that we're not buying the cows, we'll be able to save even more."

Joining them on the couch, Nicole nodded. "If he's an honorable man, he'll find a way to get the money to you. If he doesn't, then I guess that proves that you're better off without him. And Erin's right. We don't need the money. We'll be fine."

They made it sound so simple, but they hadn't considered other things, like the household expenses. Things like gas, electricity and food. Money for that didn't come out of nowhere, and it wasn't fair for her sisters to shoulder the weight.

"This isn't just about start-up costs. It's about all the expenses. How am I supposed to contribute to the running of the household?"

Erin gave her another squeeze. "I wish you would stop worrying about that. I know you think it's your duty to contribute financially, but you contribute in plenty of other ways. You take care of the boys, you cook all of our meals, you've done most of the repairs on this place, and if there's anything that needs doing, you're the first to step up to do it."

Nicole nodded. "If it were up to me and Erin to cook, we'd be eating canned soup. Thanks to you, we eat healthy, delicious meals every day. Our home is clean, in good condition and a haven for us all, and that's because of your hard work."

"You guys helped," Leah mumbled.

Nicole gave her a little nudge. "Only because you told us what to do. I know you have a lot of guilt over not contributing, but you are the very heart of this family. You keep us going. You give us the strength to carry on. To be honest, I didn't like it when you were working for Shane, because you would kill yourself working long hours over there and then come home to work even harder here. Give yourself a break. Taking care of this place is job enough."

"It's true," Erin said. "I don't know what we would do without you keeping track of everything. Back when we were in school, you told us not to count the cost. But neither of us have forgotten that if it wasn't for you and Jason working so hard, Nicole and I would have never gotten through college. You never went, because you were too busy putting us through. Let us take care of you for a change."

But she was the older sister. Wasn't taking care of them her job? It didn't seem right to sit around and do nothing. "But I have to do my share."

Erin pulled away from her and stood. Hands on hips, she hovered over her, wearing her don't-mess-with-me look. "Haven't we been telling you all the things you do for us? I know I'm technically not supposed to tell people about my clients, but, working for Ricky, I pay his bills. And he pays his housekeeper a lot more than what Nicole makes. So if you want to look at it that way, that's your share."

The disgusted noise that came from Nicole made Leah chuckle. She often bemoaned the fact that she wasn't paid nearly what she was worth, but she also knew that many of the families couldn't afford more.

"And we're not even kidding about eating canned soup all the time," Erin said. "Apparently, I can't even make mac and cheese out of a box. When I tried the other day, Dylan refused to eat it and told me that I made it wrong. How do you make it wrong?"

Leah had to laugh in spite of the seriousness of the situation. Even at a young age, her children had become quite the food snobs. They were so used to her doctoring up recipes like boxed mac and cheese, that they didn't realize that she always added a little something extra.

"I always add garlic powder. It gives it a little kick, and the extra garlic doesn't hurt as a boost to their immune system."

Erin stared at her. "Whatever. It's mac and cheese. Not gourmet. But that only proves my point. Neither of us know the difference. And I'm pretty sure that if it weren't for you forcing them down our throats at every meal, we definitely wouldn't be eating enough vegetables."

"I eat vegetables," Nicole said. "I eat lots of vegetables."

"Yeah, dipped in ranch. If it's not something Leah fixes and it's not smothered in a gallon of dressing, I've never seen you eat a vegetable."

Nicole shrugged. "So sue me for liking a little dressing with my vegetables. At least I eat them."

Her sisters' bickering made her smile. No matter how old they got, some things never changed. And even though she didn't like doing so, she'd have to admit that her sisters were right.

"I'm just disappointed about the cows. The profit margin would have allowed me to put Dylan back in therapy." She let out a long sigh. "When I was doing some research on how to help him better prepare for the coming school year, I found out that one of the therapists who wrote a book on his behavior issues lives right here in Columbine Springs. I'd seen it as the perfect opportunity to finally get Dylan some help. She's expensive, but I really love what she's written, and I've used some of her techniques already."

Nicole walked to the bench by the front door and grabbed her purse. "How much should I make the check out for?"

Leah shook her head. "No. You just got your job."

"You're impossible," Erin said, walking over to the computer. "If you won't tell us, we'll look it up online and find out ourselves. I'll be contributing, as well. Like Nicole, there is nothing more important to me than the boys' futures. How can you be so dense as to not see that? If it had been Lily, I know you would've done the same."

Her throat clogged with tears at the mention of her late niece's name. Erin never spoke of her daughter who died, whose death destroyed her marriage and, in many ways, her hope for the future. She hadn't thought that perhaps caring for the boys was a way to help Erin deal with her grief. Had Leah been too selfish in this, as well? She'd been so worried about burdening her sisters that it hadn't occurred to her that perhaps by letting her sisters help her, she was helping them.

Nicole put her arm around Erin. "I didn't think of it that way. You never speak of her, and Leah and I agreed that we wouldn't pry."

"I appreciate that. I've needed to deal with my grief in my own way. But yes, if you must know, I've found a great deal of healing by being around the boys. I like to think of myself as doing for them what I wish I could do for her. We all know that we would do anything we possibly could for our children. And I love your children like my own."

"I'll pay you back," Leah said. "Maybe once the ranch gets better established, we'll have a little extra, and you can have my share."

Nicole threw down her checkbook. "Are you kidding me? It's like you haven't been listening to us at all."

She had, and she knew she needed to do a better job at accepting her sisters' help. As she tried to think of a response, she noticed Nicole scribbling on a piece of paper.

Then Nicole handed it to her. "Based on these calculations, this is what I owe you for my college education. I can't pay it all to you now, but I can make a start."

It was a check, and when Leah looked at it, she felt sick. Her sister couldn't possibly have this kind of money. "I told you. I don't expect to be paid back."

"Then why are you being so stubborn about paying us back for what we want to do for you? For our nephews?"

The way her sister looked at her, it made her feel even more sick. She'd been hurt when her father had reduced his relationship with them to a balance sheet. In a way, that's what she was doing here. It was like a slap in the face against everything she had worked so hard for. And she was doing it to her sisters.

"I'm sorry," she said. "I didn't realize how much this meant to you. I didn't think."

Erin took the check out of Leah's hand and replaced it with another one. A blank check. "I want you to get the boys what they need. I don't want you to feel guilty for it. And you don't owe us anything. Can you please let us help you?"

Nicole took her hand. "When will you learn how much we love you? Love isn't about keeping score. You say you know that, so prove to us that you do."

Maybe in her own way, she had been keeping score. As she thought back to the lesson in First Corinthians about love not keeping a record of wrongs, she realized it probably also applied to keeping a record of rights.

She stole a glance at the Bible she'd placed on the

table beside the chair. It had been her habit to read it at night before bed while she drank her tea. It made her feel close to Helen, learning about God, seeing Helen's notes in the margins, and in a way, it had made her feel loved. Helen had done all of this for them, knowing they would never be able to repay her, simply because she loved them. She had never stopped loving them. Perhaps that was truly what love was.

When Leah was reading the Bible last night, she noticed that one of the verses Helen had highlighted said, "Greater love hath no man than this, that a man lay down his life for his friends." Next to it, Helen had written *Jesus* in big letters. But Leah couldn't help thinking that it was also about her sons. That she would be willing to do just about anything for them, including laying down her life.

Maybe she wasn't being literally asked for her life but her pride. To show her love for her sisters and her sons, she had to let go of her pride—her need to repay people for what they'd done for her—and simply accept their help. Maybe that was what love was about. And, maybe, that was really the point of what everyone had been trying to teach her about Jesus.

Love wasn't about deserving, earning or repaying. She reached for the Bible and opened it to the passage she'd read last night.

"I get it now. And I'm sorry. It didn't occur to me until now that in rejecting your help, I was rejecting your love. I'm so sorry. I love you both, and I choose to accept the love that you're offering me."

Tears ran down her face as her sisters turned and hugged her.

She didn't know how long they'd been like that when Dylan entered the room.

"What are you doing?"

She pulled away from her sisters and wiped her eyes as she looked over at her son. "I think I'm understanding for the first time what love means."

Dylan gave her a funny look. "You know what love means. What do you think you do for me and Ryan? You're the best at love of anyone I know."

She wasn't, but she wasn't going to argue with her son. She held out her arms, and he climbed into her lap.

"I love you, Dylan."

He snuggled against her. "I love you, too. Even though you're mad at Mister Shane, can I still be his friend? He said he would always be my friend."

Of course, he wouldn't give up that easily. But she still didn't know if Shane could be trusted. How else would he deceive her in the name of her best interest?

"Maybe in time," she said. "There are things I still need to work out, so you'll have to give it some time."

Her answer wasn't the sort a boy his age could understand, but he nodded anyway. "I don't like that Mister Shane made you cry."

Obviously, she hadn't done as good of a job hiding it from her son as she'd hoped. "It's grown-up stuff."

He nodded again. "I guess he's not going to be my dad after all, is he?"

No. A simple word. Two letters. Barely a sound. But she was surprised at how hard it was to make her mouth form the word.

Ryan cried out in the other room. She'd probably

have to revisit the conversation with Dylan at some point, but for now, she was grateful for the rest.

"Let's get your brother."

Dylan took her hand, and they went into the other room. While they'd miss Shane, their hearts would heal, in time. But for now, they had each other, and they always would.

Chapter Ten

Slinging bags of feed on a Saturday afternoon was not Shane's idea of a good time. Especially when it was during the town's annual Fourth of July celebration. It was one of his favorite holidays: the Saturday morning parade, the cookout at Columbine Springs Park, Old Man Perkins and his tractor pulling the train for the little ones, and the various games and activities people came up with.

And then, of course, later tonight, there would be fireworks.

He'd been hoping to experience one of his favorite parts about Columbine Springs with Leah and the boys. But since that day in the café a few weeks ago, she hadn't spoken to him nor had she returned his calls or texts. He could take a hint. In her mind, he'd done the unforgivable, even though his heart had been in the right place.

Which was why he'd volunteered to work the whole day so the other employees could enjoy the time with their families. As the new guy, it seemed only fair, but, selfishly, he was glad that he wouldn't be running into

Leah and her boys. They deserved to have a nice time today, not be reminded of something painful.

He wished he knew how Dylan had taken things. Was the little boy okay? Did he miss Shane the way Shane missed him? For all his intentions of not getting attached and reminding himself that Dylan was not his son, he still missed that little rascal and his brother like crazy.

As he lifted the last bag of feed from the cart he'd brought out from back, the front door jangled. He pulled off his gloves and stuffed them in his back pocket, then went to greet the customer.

Leah.

"What are you doing here?" he asked.

Leah let out a long sigh. "Dylan and his friend Joshua from Sunday school accidentally knocked over Miss Margaret's rabbit cage, with her prized rabbit inside, and broke the water bottle. I thought I'd run in here to see if I could find a replacement. It was an accident. They were playing soccer and missed."

She gave a tiny laugh. "But I guess it's okay, because the guy in charge of the youth soccer program saw them playing and gave me information about signing up. It'll be good to get him involved in something."

He didn't know what to say, with so much information being thrown at him at once. He hadn't expected an update on Dylan. Nice to hear the situation at church had worked out and that Dylan was making friends. Shane had been sneaking in late to church and skipping out early so he wouldn't run into Leah.

"Sounds like he's really starting to fit in," Shane said.

Leah nodded. "He is. And even though I'm still

mad at you, I suppose I should thank you for all the doors you've opened for us and for giving him more self-confidence and self-worth. Just because you did one awful thing to me doesn't make you completely evil."

Wow. She really wasn't going to let it go, was she?

Then she shook her head. "But that's not what I'm here for, though it was nice to get it off my chest. I'm doing a lot of work on my relationship with God, and as part of that, I'm trying really hard to forgive you. I know it's not the same, but I hope it counts for something."

He didn't even know how to respond. Fortunately, as he opened his mouth, hoping intelligent words came out, she shook her head.

"Don't. This isn't about you. It's about me being right with God. I can still be right with God and not be your friend. Because I don't think that will ever happen."

She looked around the feed store, then back at him. "This place is really empty. You wouldn't happen to know who works here so I can get them to help me find this rabbit-water-bottle thing I need."

He smiled as he reached for the apron he'd tossed on one of the shelves because it was getting caught on the feed display. "You're looking at him. The rabbit stuff is over here. I know what you need."

She didn't say anything as he led her to the correct area. But when they got there, she asked, "Why are you working here? Don't you have enough to do with your ranch?"

He'd promised himself not to tell her how much it had cost him to take on the cows. They were getting better now, gaining weight and showing signs of being healthy. But such news would be a sore spot for her. She'd probably see it as proof that she could have done it. But he couldn't have, not without the help of his friends and the employee discount by working here. And, of course, the extra money he made by taking on this job.

"It's a long story," he said. "But it's a good job, and I'm happy to have it."

She nodded slowly, like she was remembering that she'd once applied for this job. One more thing for her to hold against him, he supposed.

"I don't know how you do it," she said finally. "You needed my help, running a ranch. And with the extra cows, no wonder I haven't seen you around."

"I've been busy for sure." He grabbed the water bottle Leah needed and handed it to her. "This should do the trick. Miss Margaret bought one like this last week."

He was trying not to dwell on the fact that she'd noticed he hadn't been around. If she'd wanted to talk to him, she could have returned his calls.

He rang up the purchase and she left without further conversation. They'd said everything they had to. He wished it didn't hurt so much to see her again. Every day, he prayed for God to help him get over the pain. But, so far, his prayer hadn't been answered. Today's encounter made it feel fresh.

A short while later, Fred entered the store. "Take the rest of the day off," he said. "Gloria is tired of the heat, and she went home to rest. It's a shame for you to miss the festivities, and since I've had my fill, you go."

He'd have liked to argue, but Fred's expression made it clear he wouldn't hear it.

He didn't have the heart to tell Fred that he preferred working over running into Leah, who was probably having the time of her life.

Maybe he had hurt her, but at least Helen's dreams for the girls were coming true. They were settling in and making a home here in Columbine Springs.

"I ran into that lady friend of yours," Fred said. "I told her I felt bad for hiring you instead of her, but I needed someone who could be more flexible with their hours. I didn't want her thinking this was one more thing you'd stolen from her."

Great. Now he really didn't want to have to go to the town celebration.

"What did she say?"

Fred shrugged. "She's okay with it. After seeing you fight with her in the café, I figured she must be a little on the stupid side, but talking to her, she didn't seem so bad. The key with a woman like her is to not get her all riled up. You wouldn't know it to look at her, but my Gloria is the same way. Smart as a whip, gentle as a dove, but boy, if you make her mad, you'd better watch out."

"That sounds like Leah," Shane said. "I truly am sorry for hurting her, but I don't think she's ready to hear it. She told me as much when she was in here earlier."

The sage expression on Fred's face made him smile. "Sometimes you have to work out a good mad. You have to feel it before you can let it go. That's the trouble with most people these days. They pretend they're not mad, but it hangs around them like a weight they can't get rid of. Forgiveness is good, but it doesn't mean anything unless you've worked through the emotion first."

He'd have liked to take the older man's words as a sign that they could work things out. And maybe they still could. But he wasn't sure how. The more he thought about her words, the more he'd realized he had done her a great disservice. Her and her sisters. He should have talked to them. He shouldn't have put Leah in the position of convincing them of something she wasn't sure of herself. He should've gone to them and educated everyone on the situation.

At least then, he wouldn't have been stuck with a herd of cattle he wouldn't be able to sell for a while. It was an expensive mistake, both to his wallet and his heart.

Maybe someday he and Leah could talk about it.

"Now, get on with you," Fred said. "They're grilling burgers to raise money for the fire department, and I know how you like to support them. That, and Old Joe's grilling, and you're one of the few people who will eat those hockey pucks of his."

Shane chuckled. It was always good to be reminded of the things he loved about this community. In time, his wounds would heal and he wouldn't dread going out so much. He used to think that Gina leaving town was the worst way to end a relationship. But now, he wasn't so sure.

Seeing Leah today had been hard. Seeing the boys would be even more so. Would they be allowed to talk to him? Would it be all right for him to say hi? He didn't know. And he wasn't sure he wanted to. With Natalie, he could just pray for her and hope she was all right, but with the boys he could see for himself from time to time that they were. Not that he had any doubt of that fact. Leah was a good mother, and her sons would always be fine.

He left the feed store and walked the few short blocks to Columbine Springs Park. Nestled along the bank of Rock Creek, the park was bustling with activity. Folks from all over came for the Fourth of July celebration, not just locals. Food trucks were parked along the side of the road, and he spied a number of new ones. He followed the path down to where the firemen had their annual cookout to raise money to help keep the fire department going. As promised, Old Joe was manning the grill.

"It's about time you showed that ugly mug of yours around here," Old Joe said. "Come get yourself a plate. For most people, it's all-you-can-eat for five dollars, but I know how you eat, so you can give me ten."

The older man's good-natured ribbing made him smile and eased some of the tension he'd been carrying. It was well past lunch time, which meant Leah and her boys had probably already eaten. And, since they didn't realize how important the firefighters' fund-raiser was, they'd probably opted for one of the food trucks, which most likely reminded them of home.

But when he grabbed his plate and went into the pavilion, there they were.

Ryan's face was painted like a tiger, and Dylan's was painted like a wolf.

His stomach clenched, and he wanted to dump his

plate in the trash and leave. But in that moment of hesitation, Dylan noticed him.

"Mister Shane," the little boy shouted, waving.

Leah looked in his direction, and even from a distance, he could see the worry crossing her brow. She turned back and said something to Dylan, who looked chagrined.

Probably a warning not to talk to him anymore. But Dylan scooted off his bench and came toward him.

"Mom said it's okay if I invite you to come sit with us."

She did? That didn't sound like the woman he'd just talked to, but he wasn't going to argue with the little boy who looked at him with such hope in his eyes.

"That would be great. I was wondering where I was going to sit."

Dylan gave him a big smile.

"I like your face painting. You look almost like a real wolf."

"It was Joshua's idea." Dylan made a face. "I wanted to be a cowboy, but cowboys don't do any face-painting things. Mom said that if I'm really good today, she'll buy me my very own cowboy hat. Maybe you could help pick it out."

Something as simple as a cowboy hat shouldn't be a knife to his gut, but considering Shane already had one in a closet at his house that he'd picked out for Dylan that was supposed to be a reward for finishing his cowboy lessons, it felt terrible. Leah would probably tell him that he was wrong for assuming and buying it without asking her. But he'd seen it and hadn't been able to help himself. Kind of like the lonely mare in his paddock. He'd had no use for it, but it seemed the perfect horse for the boys, and it had been, for the short time they'd been with him.

When he got to the table, Leah smiled warmly at him. Almost like nothing had happened between them. What had changed?

Leah hadn't expected to see Shane so soon after talking to Fred. But her eagle-eyed son had spotted him right away. She really had no choice but to invite him over.

"Leah." He tipped his hat at her like she was any ordinary person on the street. But after knowing what he'd done...

"Mister Shane!" Even Ryan had a gleeful greeting for the man. Shane reached down and ruffled his hair, smiling.

"Are you guys having fun?"

"I tiger." Ryan pointed to his face. "Rawr!"

Shane jumped back. "Ooh, scary. You're not going to eat me, are you?"

Ryan grinned. "I only eats da bad guys. You a good guy. I no eat you."

Even her littlest boy could recognize something Leah hadn't been able to. Shane had been telling her all along that he was a good guy, but she hadn't been willing to believe him. She'd been blinded by her own pain from the past.

"I'm a wolf. Ow-oo." She had to grin at the way her son needed to show off for Shane. Her boys clearly loved him very much. And as Shane made wolf and tiger noises with her boys, her heart clenched.

Would he forgive her? She'd told him that she'd

been struggling with forgiving him, but he'd had no comment on his feelings toward her.

Nicole returned, carrying a big bag of cotton candy. "Look what I found. Who ate all their lunch?"

Both boys jumped up. "Me."

"Aunt Nicole! Mister Shane is here."

At Dylan's excited exclamation, Nicole turned and gave Shane one of her famous glares. Leah hadn't had time to discuss matters with her sister. She didn't know about the conversation Leah had had with Fred.

As Nicole opened the bag containing the cotton candy, the boys quickly forgot about Mister Shane and ran to their aunt.

"Nicole, the fishing derby is about to start. Would you mind taking the boys, and I'll catch up?"

The women exchanged glances, and Nicole nodded. Holding out her hand, she said, "Come on, boys. Who wants to catch a fish?"

Once they had scampered off, Leah turned to Shane.

He took a step back. "I know. I did my best to keep my distance from them. I'm not trying to be disrespectful to you or your parenting. They're your boys, and you have every right to say who gets to be with them."

It was hard avoiding a person in such a small town. She'd thought that they would end up running into each other at church, but she seemed to miss him coming and going. Still, it was inevitable that they would see one another. And Shane would obviously encounter her sons.

To her surprise, at this moment, she found herself happy to see him. Because after running into Fred when she left the feed store, she owed him a huge apology.

"It's okay. I might have been a little too harsh with you. In fact, I was hoping we could talk."

It was harder than she'd expected to admit how wrong she'd been, especially when Shane looked at her so suspiciously.

"I don't know if that's a good idea," he said.

"If not now, can we please set a date?" She hoped she sounded like a kinder, gentler version of herself, someone he wouldn't be afraid to talk to.

Shane nodded slowly. "We can take a walk by the river if you like."

He still had a plate of food in his hand.

"Don't you want to eat first? I don't mind waiting." She gestured at her own empty plate. "I need to clean up, so eat. And then I'm happy to wait for you to be done."

He gave her a slight nod, then sat at one of the benches the boys had vacated. He still looked as though he thought she might go off on him at any minute, and she didn't blame him. After all, she hadn't given him much reason to think anything different.

She let him eat in silence as she cleaned up after the boys. Lingering over the trash can, she wanted to give Shane the space he needed to finish his meal in peace, but she also wanted to give herself the chance to collect her thoughts and formulate what she was going to say to him.

In the past, her prayers had been half-hearted attempts at talking to a God she wasn't sure existed. But now, she knew He was real. And she knew He was listening. *Lord, please help me find the words.*

I'm not asking for everything to be magically all right between us, nor do I expect that things will be perfect. But I want us to hear each other out.

Her heart felt lighter as she returned to Shane. He was just finishing his hamburger.

"I'll take you to a spot I know, where it's less crowded," he said.

He'd asked her for privacy when they'd had their argument in the café. But she hadn't listened. She'd been too angry. Whatever came of this conversation, she would pay attention to what he wanted.

They walked past the crowd and down the trail along the river. She'd never been this way before, not wanting to let her sons get so near the water. Neither boy could swim, and the idea of being that close to such a fast-moving creek would have been too tempting for them.

They came around the bend, where there was a bench. Shane gestured to it. "I don't think we'll be disturbed here. It's a popular place for people to walk, but with everyone so busy at the Fourth of July festivities, I doubt anyone will come upon us."

Leah took a deep breath as they sat. This was the moment of truth.

"I owe you an apology," she said.

He nodded. "You mentioned wanting to talk."

"I talked to Fred today. I was trying to be pleasant, so I made a little joke about him hiring someone. I think he thought I was mad, even though I wasn't. He was quick to tell me that he didn't hire me because of my lack of availability. But he also told me off over how I had ruined you."

He looked at the ground but didn't say anything.

"Is it true? It hurt your finances to hire me? And took everything you had to buy those cows? And to keep paying for their care, you had to get a job?"

He looked over at her. "Yes."

His voice was barely a whisper, like he hadn't wanted to admit it.

"You risked everything to save us. Fred said those cows were in awful shape."

"I did what I had to do." Shifting his weight, he moved closer to her. "But I was wrong in how I did it. You were right. I should have talked to you. I shouldn't have only put the burden on your shoulders, when your sisters had a role in the decision-making process, as well. I should have gotten you all together and explained my concerns."

He sounded sincere, but more than that, he sounded truly regretful that he had made the mistakes he'd made.

But he wasn't the only one to make mistakes. "And I should have been more willing to hear you out rather than jumping to conclusions. I got so used to being lied to, so used to men who took advantage of me and the women I love. I'd forgotten there were good people in this world. I'm sorry. And I'm sorry for comparing you with those other men. I should have judged you on your own merits."

He held his hand out to her like he wanted her to take it, so she did. He gave her hand a squeeze. "We both made a lot of mistakes. I know you said you were struggling with forgiving me, so I hope that this conversation will lead us both to forgiving each other. Can we start fresh?"

Leah nodded. "I'd like that."

She squeezed his hand, and it felt good to be close to him. But after what she'd been reading in her Bible, and what Fred had told her, it wasn't enough.

"Do you remember that day in church, when the pastor talked about First Corinthians? What that meant about love?"

He nodded.

"I read something else, too. In John. About there not being any greater love than being willing to lay down your life for your friends."

Shane nodded again. "I'm happy to hear that you're reading your Bible. It would've meant the world to Helen."

"Actually, it's Helen's Bible. I found it. As I've been reading it, I've realized how much of a disservice I've been doing you. You've shown me love in all the ways First Corinthians has said, but you've also shown me the greatest love. You were willing to risk everything you had to save me. To save my family. Most people would've walked away and left us to our ignorance. And if we made a stupid decision, it would have been on us. But you wanted more for us. You wanted more for me." Tears filled her eyes as she realized the sacrifice Shane had made for her.

"It was the right thing to do. I couldn't see you get hurt, but, in my idiocy and stubbornness, you were hurt anyway. I can't tell you how sorry I am."

She no longer wanted to dwell on their regrets. Instead, she hoped to move forward.

"But did you do it because you cared for me? Because you love me?"

He looked at the ground. "Yes, but I wasn't as good at showing you love as I should have been. I should have been more patient with you instead of taking matters into my own hands."

Leah leaned into him. "Wasn't it you who told me that because we're human, we all make mistakes? I just need to know—if love was your motivation in those decisions, have I ruined it? Or is there a chance for us to try again?"

He finally looked over at her, pulling away slightly. "I don't want you thinking you have to try at a relationship with me because of all I've done for you."

It hadn't occurred to her that he would feel that way or think that her feelings for him weren't genuine. But after her conversations with her sisters and the changes they'd made, she could see why he would think that.

"It's true that I once saw love as a balance sheet. But my sisters set me straight. When someone does something for you out of love, you don't owe them anything, and if they say otherwise, then it's not real love. I'm only interested in real love. So, if you say I owe you nothing, then I know you love me, and I am content with that."

She couldn't make out his expression, so she took a deep breath.

"I'm not working, nor am I looking for a job. My sisters want to show me their love by letting me stay home with the boys. They say I do enough around the house that I don't need to contribute financially. They are even paying for Dylan and his therapy. I'm learning that love isn't just about giving but about being willing to receive."

He nodded slowly. "Dylan is in therapy?"

"Yes. One of the authors of a book that has been very helpful to me lives nearby. I was able to get him into therapy with her, a lot sooner than I had planned. I originally wanted to use the profit from the sale of the cattle to pay for it, but my sisters took money from their savings so we could do it now. There's nothing more important to them than my son's well-being."

He put his arm around her. "It's been hard for you, hasn't it? You take care of everyone else, and it's hard for you to accept being taken care of."

She nodded. He had it right.

Shane gave her a squeeze. "I'm proud of you. It's one of the reasons I can't help loving you. You're constantly seeking to do better and be better. You're a wonderful sister, mother and friend."

The expression on his face warmed her heart. And made her feel…

But he wasn't done yet.

"I love you. Is that what you needed to hear me say?"

Until now, she hadn't thought she needed the words. But with as many misunderstandings as had been between them, it was good to have it all cleared up.

"Thank you." Then she took a moment to laugh at herself. "That's probably not the right way to respond to someone's declaration of love. But I know how hard I made it to be loved. You are strong enough to love me through even my worst moments. And even though I know I should say 'I love you' back, I don't know that it's a strong enough word to express how I truly feel about you. But I do love you."

He took her in his arms and gave her a gentle kiss. "You've got it all wrong. You've been very easy to love. For as many times as I told myself that loving you wasn't the right thing, that it would be too hard, too complicated, I couldn't help it. There were too many other reasons for me to love you anyway. You're a good woman, and you probably don't hear that often enough."

Receiving Shane's love was an overwhelming feeling, because she knew she didn't deserve it, and yet he loved her anyway. But that was the point of love.

"I'm so sorry for all the ways I pushed you away. And for accusing you without listening to your side."

He pulled her closer to him . "So, we're back to that, are we? What about me? I stormed into your life and took over in areas where I should have included you as my full partner. That's not love. But you've chosen me anyway. So, let's stop with all the apologies and promise that, in the future, we will both do better about communicating and trusting each other."

That was probably the biggest lesson in love. But it was also one of the biggest points they learned about in First Corinthians. Not keeping a record of wrongs but pressing on and continuing to do right by one another.

His eyes searched her face, like he was looking to unlock all her secrets. And she didn't want to keep any from him.

But there was one more thing they still had to resolve. "Maybe it's a little presumptuous of me, but I know a little boy who really wants you to be his daddy. We said we weren't going to make this about the kids, but I know they've been hurting, too. They miss you. I've missed you. If we're going to do this, then let's just commit to doing it."

Shane grinned. "Was that a proposal?"

She'd be lying if she said she wanted anything different. But they'd barely gotten back together. "I hope

for that in our future. But I want to do things right. I
saw the church is doing a small group for soon-to-be-
engaged, engaged and married couples. I'd really like
you to go with me. We both made a lot of mistakes in
the relationships we've had over the years, and I want
to do this one right."

When he pulled her into another kiss, it was like
coming home. Like everything in her life fit perfectly
together, and the world didn't feel so heavy anymore.
But just as he deepened the kiss, a voice rang out.

"Mister Shane! What are you doing kissing my
mom again?"

Instead of looking happy, the little boy ran over to
him and kicked him in the shin. "You can't do that to
my mom unless you marry her." Then he kicked him
again. "And I'm not sure I should let you because you
made her cry."

That was the trouble with trying to have a relationship while raising two boys. She and Dylan hadn't
talked much about the day she came home crying, and
she hadn't wanted to push or pry. But maybe, given
her son's level of anger, she should have.

"Hey, buddy, calm down." Shane held his arms out
to Dylan.

Dylan's face reddened. "You're my friend, Mister Shane. But you also made my mom cry. And now
you're kissing her. You told me cowboys have to protect people. I'm asking you, as a cowboy—you leave
my mom alone. If you make her cry again, we can't
be friends anymore."

The backs of her eyes stung with tears at her son's
words, but she willed herself to keep them inside.
She didn't want him to see, not now. Not when he

was doing his very best to protect her. He'd grown a lot, and even though it was wrong for him to approach Shane with such violence, it showed that he was learning to think of others and care for them in a deeper way.

Shane seemed to understand that, as well. He patted Leah's leg. "I did hurt your mom, and I did make her cry. But that's what we're talking about now, and we're working it out. I hurt her feelings, and I'm learning how to do better."

Dylan looked at him suspiciously. "My dad used to make her cry."

"I know. And I'm working very hard not to hurt her like that. Your mom is a special lady, and she deserves to be loved."

Nicole had come up behind Leah and placed her hand on her shoulder. Ryan climbed into her lap. "*My* mama."

In a way, she felt sorry for Shane, having to face her family. The only one who was missing was Erin, but she'd been commandeered to man the church booth for a while.

Shane turned to Ryan and smiled. "She is your mama, but she's also a very special lady to me. Can we both love her?"

The gesture was sweet but completely lost on a two-year-old. Ryan answered by snuggling back up to Leah as she put her arms around him and gave him a good squeeze.

Dylan stepped between Leah and Shane. "How do I know you're not going to hurt her again?"

Little boys shouldn't have to be their mother's protectors, and she started to crane her neck to look at

Nicole to see how she should handle this. Her sister seemed to sense her hesitation and gave her a little squeeze on the shoulders to reassure her.

Shane scooted over and gave the bench a pat. "That's a good question, and I'm glad you asked. Loving someone is hard, and sometimes we accidentally hurt each other without meaning to. It's because we're all different, with different ideas and different ways of looking at the world. But love is about working through it, which is what your mom and I are trying to do. Has your mom ever hurt you?"

The question made Leah's insides quake. Not because she had anything to hide, but she still remembered how upset her son had been when the authorities had asked him the same question.

Dylan climbed on to the bench. "Not like my dad or some of the kids at my old school. She would never hurt anyone like that."

Nicole gave her shoulders another squeeze, like she knew how hard it was for her to sit through this. She didn't believe Shane would fit in that category, either, but it hadn't occurred to her that Dylan might have thought so.

"I would never hurt your mom like that. I would never hurt anyone like that. It's not what a cowboy does."

Dylan glanced over at her, then back at Shane. "She was crying like she used to when my dad would hurt her."

One more thing that hadn't occurred to her. She'd always fought with Jason in private, when the boys weren't around. But clearly Dylan had heard her, and even though Jason had never physically harmed her,

Dylan assumed he had. She reached up and gave her sister's hand a squeeze. At least now they could share this information with Dylan's counselor and help him work through the issue.

"Mister Shane didn't hurt me like that," Leah said, removing her hand from Nicole's and putting her arm around her son. "He made me sad, it's true. And then I got mad. So mad that I needed a break. Does that ever happen to you?"

She knew the answer, which was why she asked. Hopefully, Dylan would come up with the answer for himself and see the connection.

At first, Dylan's face scrunched up like it did when he wasn't sure. But then he nodded. "Like when all the mad inside me is really, really big and I don't know what to do."

She nodded. "That's exactly what it felt like for me. I needed time to cool off. But I took too long, because once I realized how sad I was about things between me and Shane, I didn't know what to do. I knew I had been wrong, not giving him a chance to talk to me, and I didn't know how to say I was sorry."

Recognition washed over Dylan's face as he processed her words. She tried to keep her language familiar to him, because this was exactly what he'd been talking about with his therapist. How to manage anger, not bottling it up or acting out. But taking the time to cool down, then dealing with the emotion.

"I didn't like that Mister Shane made you cry, but today when I saw him, I forgot about it, because I love him. When I saw him kissing you, I remembered. I don't want him to make you cry again. I don't like it when you're sad."

She pulled her son close again, the movement awkward with Ryan in her arms. A fact which Ryan expressed great displeasure over as he wiggled free. "I go play."

"I'll take care of it," Nicole said, chasing after him.

Dylan turned his attention back to Shane. "Doctor Maggie says I shouldn't hurt people when I'm mad. I'm sorry for kicking you."

Shane held out his arms. "I'm sorry for making you think you had to protect her. It seems you're learning your cowboy lessons really well. You're going to make a good cowboy. But how about you leave grown-up stuff between me and your mom to me?"

Dylan glanced over at her. Then back at Shane. "Someone needs to protect her."

How had she missed that her son thought it was his job? One more thing for them to talk about with Maggie. Crazy that her relationship difficulties with Shane would cause something to open up in her son so she could better understand how his mind worked and how she needed to help him.

One more blessing she hadn't expected.

"I promise your mom is a strong enough woman to protect herself. But I know, if she ever needs help, she's also strong enough that she will let us know so we can be there for her. Sometimes, you have to let people work it out on their own."

His answer seemed to please Dylan, who hopped off the bench. "We better go make sure Ryan didn't get Aunt Nicole to take him on another train ride without me."

Then, in a gesture that he had to have copied from all the times she done so to him, Dylan put his hands on his hips and stared at Shane. "And you better not think about kissing my mom again until you make an honest woman of her."

She resisted the urge to giggle. An honest woman? Where had he even heard that?

But Shane took her son's words to heart. "I have every intention of doing the right thing by your mom. But can you give us a chance to work on it?"

Dylan looked thoughtful for a moment, like he was weighing the need to protect her again.

"It's okay, I've got this," Leah told him, standing and holding out her hand. "How about you just work on being friends with Shane and more of your cowboy lessons, and let me figure out the other stuff?"

He looked doubtful and didn't take her hand.

"Remember what Doctor Maggie said about you needing to be a kid and not worrying about the grown-ups' problems?"

Dylan nodded. All right.

Shane stood. "How about we leave all this stuff behind, and we catch up with your brother and Aunt Nicole so we can ride the train?"

Even though the train was a powerful motivation, Dylan squared his shoulders in the best little-boy way he could and marched up to Shane. "You be good to my mom."

"I will, cowboy."

Dylan gave a swift nod as he took his mother's hand. "Let's go."

Shane came around the other side of Leah and slipped his hand in hers. It felt right, holding hands with the man she loved and her son. And even though

Dylan had been so protective a few moments ago, he didn't object to the gesture.

The three of them walked back to the park in search of Nicole and Ryan. Ryan was on the swings, laughing like he didn't have a care in the world. Dylan ran toward him. "Come on. Let's ride the train."

"Twain!" Ryan shouted.

Once they got the boys gathered, they went in search of the tractor-pulled train that had been such a hit with the boys.

Nicole grabbed Leah and gave her a quick hug. "I'm assuming something big must've happened to make you so open to Shane and letting him be around the boys. For what it's worth, even though I think he was wrong with what he did with the cows, I still believe he's a good man. Let yourself be happy. You deserve it."

With a final squeeze, Nicole said, "And now I've got to see a man about a horse." She giggled. "I've heard that in movies and always wanted to say that. And guess what? It's true. I think I finally found the perfect horse for us."

As she skipped off, Leah was happy to see her sister so hopeful. Just like with finding the cows, finding the right horse for the family was proving to be difficult. But like all things she'd learned about the ranch, Leah believed that that, too, would come in time.

"What was that about?" Shane asked, coming up alongside Leah.

"I think you just got my sister's blessing, so long as you don't mess it up."

She kept her tone light, and Shane gave her a soft nudge. "So long as *you* don't mess it up."

They laughed and walked hand in hand, following the boys as they ran toward the train. Once she got the boys settled in their cars and off on the ride, she let out a contented sigh.

A day like this was what she'd always wanted for her family. But having Shane here to share it with made it all the more joyful.

Maybe Helen hadn't been able to be a part of their lives for as long as Leah would have liked. But she was still with them in spirit, and because she'd never given up on loving them, their lives were now full of blessings they could have never imagined.

Shane pulled her closer to him. "A penny for your thoughts."

She looked up at him and smiled. "They're worth a whole lot more than a penny. More like a ranch. And even then, I'm not sure you could put a price tag on them. Because the depth of love the Bible teaches us about is priceless, and I'm so grateful to have experienced it, thanks to Helen and thanks to you."

He gently cupped her chin, then kissed her on top of her head. "Knowing Helen, she would say that all of the hardship she went through in life was worth it to have you say that. And I hope you know, that's how I feel about loving you."

Despite her son's explicit warnings for them not to kiss again, Leah couldn't help straightening to her tiptoes to give Shane a kiss. Just a little one, but enough for him to know how much she loved him. "I do know now. And it feels like coming home."

Epilogue

They'd been riding in Shane's truck over rough terrain for longer than Leah's nerves would have liked. But when they arrived at the expansive land before them, with mountains peeking in the distance, she couldn't complain. The scenery was breathtaking. Even the boys, who'd started to get cranky, seemed to know this was a special place.

"Come on, guys, we're here." Shane's voice sounded as excited as it had Christmas morning, when he'd invited them over to his house.

He'd had special presents for them all, including a cowboy hat for Dylan. Which Dylan basically never took off unless it was improper to be wearing one. He'd probably sleep in it, too, if she would let him. That, and the cowboy boots Shane had gotten them. Both boys wore theirs with pride, saying they were just like Mister Shane.

Once they all got out of the truck and were standing at the fence, Leah noticed the cows in the distance. And they had clearly noticed them, too. Because they were all coming toward them. Now that she was back working with Shane, Leah knew this meant the cows thought they were getting fed. Unfortunately, there wasn't more than the extra bale of hay Shane always kept in the back of his truck. Not nearly enough to feed these beasts.

One of the cows in particular came toward them, and Shane immediately climbed the fence and went over to her. He patted her and stroked her neck. He'd always told them that cows were not pets, but this cow seemed to be a favorite of his.

"What are you doing, petting that cow like a dog?" she asked.

Shane grinned. "This one is special. Her name is Petunia, and she and I have a special bond. You remember those cows that caused so many problems between us?"

Leah nodded. Even though they'd resolved their differences about the herd, they'd agreed, after Leah talked to the vet, that that herd was not for her to learn on. So she'd let it go and focused mainly on working with Shane's healthy cows, learning about them and tending to the ones who became ill from time to time.

"Well, Petunia was one of the sickest ones. I only ended up losing four head, but there were a lot of times I thought I would lose Petunia. When things looked most hopeless between you and me, Petunia was who I talked to about it. And I told her, that if she made it through and you forgave me, I would invite her to our wedding."

Leah stared at him. He did not just tell her he'd invited a cow to their wedding. Not that they had one planned. She knew they'd plan the future together, and for now, it was enough. Though her sisters teasing her about it was starting to get old.

"Come meet her," Shane said. "You too, boys."

"I pet a cow." Ryan's joyful laugh made her smile. He'd just turned three, too young to really know what he was going to do with his life, but given the joy he found in petting the animals, she knew he would someday end up working with them. Maybe he would be taking over the family ranch.

Dylan gave Leah a small shove in the direction of the fence. "Mom. She's just a cow. She's not going to bite."

She glanced at her son, who certainly looked like he was scheming again. She'd handled plenty of cows and knew they wouldn't bite. Once she and Shane had been together for six months and their relationship was looking stable, Dylan had started once again making noises about wanting Shane to be his dad. And as many times as both adults reminded him that it was a grown-up situation, it didn't stop her son from continuing to ask.

Therapy had done wonders for Dylan, and she and Shane had joined in on a few of the sessions. She wished it had been something she'd done with Jason, not necessarily because she thought it would have changed the outcome, but maybe she would've been better able to handle the situation. Now, she felt she had the skills to deal with her relationship issues as well as handle the things from her past that still bubbled up. Most important, she'd seen the growth in her son and was grateful.

She climbed the fence, then she and Dylan helped Ryan through. When they got to Shane, Leah was pleased to see how well her boys were following the rules. They'd learned not to run or shout and to listen to Shane's instructions.

"It's all right, you can come close to her. Unlike most cows, she's not afraid of humans. The vet says it's because she bonded to me. And she's one hundred percent healthy. As a matter of fact, they've all been given a clean bill of health and show no sign of disease."

Leah, Shane and the boys approached, taking turns to pet the cow.

"What's that around her neck?" Leah asked, reaching for what appeared to be a ribbon. She was starting to learn that Shane had a little bit of sentimentality in him, but she hadn't expected that he would put a ribbon around a cow's neck.

But then she noticed what was on the ribbon.

An engagement ring hung from it, glistening in the sunlight.

"That's for you," Shane said. "Actually, they're all for you. Back in the old days, there were dowries and such, and many a man traded his cattle for a good woman. So I'm giving all these cows to you. You're a good woman, and I wanted to give you a symbol, not only of my love, but of my absolute faith in you."

He was giving her cows? Granted, there was an engagement ring dangling from the ribbon on the cow's neck, but cows?

They'd talked about marriage, but seeing the ring made her chest tighten in a funny way and brought tears to her eyes.

Shane got down on one knee. "I promised Petunia that when the time was right, I would ask you to marry me. I talked with your boys and asked their permission, right after I talked to your sisters. But, ultimately, the choice is yours. Will you be my wife?"

Tears ran down her face as she saw the love shining in Shane's eyes. She reached over and took the ribbon off the cow, handing it to Shane. "Will you put it on me?"

He stood and slipped the ring onto her finger. It was a perfect fit. Dylan brought his brother around to Shane. "Does this mean we can stop calling you Mister Shane? Because me and Ryan have been talking, and we really want to call you Dad."

At three, Ryan was hardly the conversationalist. But, as though he could sense her thoughts, he turned to Shane and said, "Dad."

When Shane scooped the little boy up in his arms, there were tears in his eyes. "Your mom hasn't said yes yet."

Leah held her hand out to her son. "I couldn't think of anything I want more. Yes, I will marry you."

And even though Shane still held Ryan, and Dylan had his arms around them, she stepped up and kissed her fiancé. They were family now, and being together felt right.

But the kiss was over too soon, with Ryan squirming in Shane's arms. Shane set the little boy down, and Dylan held his hand out to him. "Let's go over there and pick some flowers for Mom. We can give the grown-ups a little privacy."

He sounded so mature, so wise. When Leah glanced at him, he tipped his hat at her just like Shane did. A year ago, he would have thrown a fit at the idea of keeping his brother occupied for a few minutes so the adults could have a moment to themselves, but as she watched Dylan help Ryan up after stumbling over a rock or something, her heart filled with pride at how much her son had grown.

Between therapy, going to church and having the example of a good man who loved him, Dylan was thriving. And Leah had learned that love really was about seeing things long-term.

Everything from their Bible studies was true. Love was patient, being willing to see it through for the long term. Love was kind. Love was...

Before she could finish the thought, Shane's arms came around her, and he gave her a proper kiss. Everything she'd learned about love during her time here in Columbine Springs was embodied in this one moment with the man who proved that there was such a thing as love like that.

Unfortunately, even with Dylan taking his brother away, there was still one distraction. Petunia let out a long moo to remind them that she was still there.

But that was life on the ranch. And she wouldn't have it any other way.

* * * * *

*If you loved this tale of Western romance,
be sure to check out these other
stories of Western romance*

The Rancher's Unexpected Baby
by Jill Lynn
A Cowboy In Shepherd's Crossing
by Ruth Logan Herne
Her Cowboy's Twin Blessings
by Patricia Johns
Beneath Montana Skies
by Mia Ross

Available now from Love Inspired!

Find more great reads at www.LoveInspired.com.

Dear Reader,

One of the things I've been thinking about a lot is what it means to love one another. The theme verse for this story—1 Corinthians 13, verses 4-8 and 13—has been on my mind a lot lately, especially as I look at how I love the others in my life. Leah has learned to see love as being one way, Shane another, and it took them being reminded about what the Bible says about love to truly understand how to love one another. Sometimes, we get our minds set on what we think love means—what has to happen in our lives to feel loved. And yet, so much of how we measure love isn't how we're supposed to measure love at all. Even though I know I don't always do it right, I'm so grateful that God sees my heart and chooses to love me anyway. I pray that you, too, will know the kind of love Jesus teaches us about in the Bible.

I love connecting with my readers, so be sure to find me online:

Newsletter *eepurl.com/7HCXj*
Website *danicafavorite.com*
Twitter *Twitter.com/danicafavorite*
Instagram *Instagram.com/danicafavorite*
Facebook *Facebook.com/DanicaFavoriteAuthor*
Facebook Reader Group *Facebook.com/groups/DanicaFavorite/*
Amazon *Amazon.com/Danica-Favorite/e/B00K RP0IFU*
BookBub bookbub.com/authors/danica-favorite

Sending love and prayers to you and yours,
Danica Favorite

COMING NEXT MONTH FROM
Love Inspired®

Available February 19, 2019

THE AMISH BACHELOR'S BABY
Amish Spinster Club • by Jo Ann Brown

Finally following his dreams of opening a bakery, Caleb Hartz hires Annie Wagler as his assistant. But they both get more than they bargain for when his runaway teenage cousin and her infant son arrive. Can they work together to care for mother and child—without falling in love?

THE AMISH BAKER
by Marie E. Bast

When his son breaks one of baker Sarah Gingerich's prized possessions, widower Caleb Brenneman insists the boy make amends by doing odd jobs in her bake shop. While the child draws them together, can they ever overcome their differing Amish beliefs and become the perfect family?

RANCHER TO THE RESCUE
Three Brothers Ranch • by Arlene James

Coming to the aid of a woman in her broken-down car, Jake Smith doesn't expect to find the answer to his childcare problems. But Kathryn Stepp needs a job and the widower needs a nanny for his son. And their business arrangement might just develop into so much more.

HER LAST CHANCE COWBOY
Big Heart Ranch • by Tina Radcliffe

With a new job at Big Heart Ranch, pregnant single mom Hannah Vincent is ready for a fresh start. But as she and her boss, horse trainer Tripp Walker, grow closer, Hannah can't help but wonder if she's prepared for a new love.

HIS SECRET DAUGHTER
by Lisa Carter

When ex-soldier Jake McAbee learns he has a daughter, he's determined to raise the little girl. But can he win his daughter's trust and convince Callie Jackson—the child's foster mother—that the best place for Maisie is with him?

SEASON OF HOPE
by Lisa Jordan

Jake Holland needs a piece of land for his farming program for disabled veterans—but his ex-wife owns it. So they strike a deal: she'll sell him the land if he renovates her home. But can they resolve their past—and long-kept secrets—for a second chance?

LICNM0219

Get 4 FREE REWARDS!

We'll send you 2 FREE Books plus 2 FREE Mystery Gifts.

Love Inspired® books feature contemporary inspirational romances with Christian characters facing the challenges of life and love.

FREE Value Over $20

YES! Please send me 2 FREE Love Inspired® Romance novels and my 2 FREE mystery gifts (gifts are worth about $10 retail). After receiving them, if I don't wish to receive any more books, I can return the shipping statement marked "cancel." If I don't cancel, I will receive 6 brand-new novels every month and be billed just $5.24 for the regular-print edition or $5.74 each for the larger-print edition in the U.S., or $5.74 each for the regular-print edition or $6.24 each for the larger-print edition in Canada. That's a savings of at least 13% off the cover price. It's quite a bargain! Shipping and handling is just 50¢ per book in the U.S. and 75¢ per book in Canada.* I understand that accepting the 2 free books and gifts places me under no obligation to buy anything. I can always return a shipment and cancel at any time. The free books and gifts are mine to keep no matter what I decide.

Choose one: ☐ **Love Inspired® Romance**
Regular-Print
(105/305 IDN GMY4)

☐ **Love Inspired® Romance**
Larger-Print
(122/322 IDN GMY4)

Name (please print)

Address   Apt. #

City   State/Province   Zip/Postal Code

Mail to the **Reader Service:**
IN U.S.A.: P.O. Box 1341, Buffalo, NY 14240-8531
IN CANADA: P.O. Box 603, Fort Erie, Ontario L2A 5X3

Want to try 2 free books from another series? Call 1-800-873-8635 or visit www.ReaderService.com.

---

*Terms and prices subject to change without notice. Prices do not include sales taxes, which will be charged (if applicable) based on your state or country of residence. Canadian residents will be charged applicable taxes. Offer not valid in Quebec. This offer is limited to one order per household. Books received may not be as shown. Not valid for current subscribers to Love Inspired Romance books. All orders subject to approval. Credit or debit balances in a customer's account(s) may be offset by any other outstanding balance owed by or to the customer. Please allow 4 to 6 weeks for delivery. Offer available while quantities last.

Your Privacy—The Reader Service is committed to protecting your privacy. Our Privacy Policy is available online at www.ReaderService.com or upon request from the Reader Service. We make a portion of our mailing list available to reputable third parties that offer products we believe may interest you. If you prefer that we not exchange your name with third parties, or if you wish to clarify or modify your communication preferences, please visit us at www.ReaderService.com/consumerschoice or write to us at Reader Service Preference Service, P.O. Box 9062, Buffalo, NY 14240-9062. Include your complete name and address.

LI19R

Finally following his dreams of opening a bakery, Caleb Hartz hires Annie Wagler as his assistant. But they both get more than they bargain for when his runaway teenage cousin and her infant son arrive. Can they work together to care for mother and child— without falling in love?

Read on for a sneak preview of
The Amish Bachelor's Baby *by Jo Ann Brown, available February 2019 from Love Inspired!*

"I wanted to talk to you about a project I'm getting started on. I'm opening a bakery."

"You are?" Annie couldn't keep the surprise out of her voice.

"Ja," Caleb said. "I stopped by to see if you'd be interested in working for me."

"You want to hire me? To work in your bakery?"

"I've had some success selling bread and baked goods at the farmers' market in Salem. Having a shop will allow me to sell year-round, but I can't be there every day and do my work at the farm. My sister Miriam told me you'd do a *gut* job for me."

"It sounds intriguing," Annie said. "What would you expect me to do?"

"Tend the shop and handle customers. There would be some light cleaning. I may need you to help with baking sometimes."

"Ja, I'd be interested in the job."

"Then it's yours. If you've got time now, I'll give you a tour of the bakery, and we can talk more about what I'd need you to do."

"Gut." The wind buffeted her, almost knocking her from her feet.

She mumbled that she needed to let her twin, Leanna, know where she was going. He wrapped his arms around himself as another blast of wind struck them.

"Hurry…anna…" The wind swallowed the rest of his words as she rushed toward the house.

She halted midstep.

Anna?

Had Caleb thought he was talking to her twin? She'd clear everything up on their way to the bakery. She wanted the job. It was an answer to so many prayers, for God to let her find a way to help her sister be happy again, happy as Leanna had been before the man she loved married someone else without telling her.

Leanna was attracted to Caleb, and he'd be a fine match for her. Outgoing where her twin was quiet. A well-respected, handsome man whose *gut* looks would be the perfect foil for her twin's. But Leanna would be too shy to let Caleb know she was interested in him. That was where Annie could help.

As she was rushing to the house, she reminded herself of one vital thing. She must be careful not to let her own attraction to Caleb grow while they worked together.

That might be the hardest part of the job.

Don't miss
The Amish Bachelor's Baby *by Jo Ann Brown,*
available February 2019 wherever
Love Inspired® books and ebooks are sold.

www.LoveInspired.com

LIEXP0219

Inspirational Romance to Warm Your Heart and Soul

Join our social communities to connect with other readers who share your love!

Sign up for the Love Inspired newsletter at **www.LoveInspired.com** to be the first to find out about upcoming titles, special promotions and exclusive content.

CONNECT WITH US AT:

Facebook.com/groups/HarlequinConnection

 Facebook.com/LoveInspiredBooks

 Twitter.com/LoveInspiredBks

LISOCIAL2018